*What happens when you run into
everything you've been running from?*

# What others are saying about *Cliff Falls*

"Can a novel heal your image of God and yourself? *Cliff Falls* has the potential to do just that. Flavored by remarkable wit, this adventure will nourish your soul. It is that good!"

- **BOBBY SCHULLER**, LEAD PASTOR, *HOUR OF POWER*

"Ditto to what Bobby said! Thank you for a palpable, gritty experience of redemption. So real. Art reflecting life. Well done!"

- **AMY GRANT**, GRAMMY AWARD-WINNING SINGER AND SONGWRITER

"When C.B. Shiepe writes about God, he is on such familiar turf that he is able to capture the nuance and depth of that relationship, bringing the reader into his personal sphere, and providing an experience to build on."

- **EDWARD GRINNAN**, EDITOR-IN-CHIEF, *GUIDEPOSTS*

"A stunningly visual journey told with wit and humor that is anchored with a big heart and tons of soul. *Cliff Falls* reads with ease and confidence, and has dialogue as fresh as your last conversation. This book will make a difference in your life."

- **SARAH SKIBITZKE**, EMMY AWARD-WINNING PRODUCER, A&E *INTERVENTION*

"*Cliff Falls* is above all a very human story, rich in feeling, wide in the apparent randomness of experience, full of injured, lost people, and hungry for true human freedom and hope. Underneath and through it all is the underpinning of grace that never lets go and holds the final word. The power of empathy and love changes everything."

- **MARK LABBERTON**, PRESIDENT, FULLER THEOLOGICAL SEMINARY

"The Best of the Best. The Bestselling Independently Published Book in the 125 year history of Vroman's Bookstore."

- **VROMAN'S BOOKSTORE**, PASADENA, CALIFORNIA

"Identity is a fragile subject. Often we can't know who we really are until we peel off the masks we wear out of our need for acceptance or fear of rejection. Rooted in the silent bedrock of the One who calls us by our true name, this transformative book provides a way forward for all of us who have forgotten who we really are. Thank you, C.B. Shiepe."

- **JEREMY RIVERA**, FOUNDER, LITTLE J FILMS

"Selecting *Cliff Falls* for Arcadia's One Community, One Book program proved to be an inspiration for a whole city. A catalyst for healing: Everyone should read this life-affirming novel."

- **SCOTT HETTRICK**, C.E.O., ARCADIA CHAMBER OF COMMERCE, *HOLLYWOODINHIDEF.COM*

"I believe in *Cliff Falls*, the best fictional rendition of the kid actor saga I've ever read. I sat up through the dark hours reading this book. It kept me turning the pages...and filled me with a sense of hope. As an advocate and former child star, I highly recommend this illuminating and insightful work. There are so many layers in this novel. I promise you this is an enriching experience."

- **PAUL PETERSEN**, FOUNDER, A MINOR CONSIDERATION / *THE DONNA REED SHOW*

"A fast, cinematic read, I recognized myself in *Cliff Falls*. The pressure to perform and to be someone other than who we want to be is universal. C.B. Shiepe has captured that experience and married it to our celebrity-centric culture. This entertaining, insightful book is the engaging result."

- **CHARLES SLOCUM**, WRITERS GUILD OF AMERICA WEST

"Shiepe's writing is rich. The dialogue is natural, leaving space for the reader to feel hurt, fear, and hope throughout the story. What isn't said is as important as what is said. Shiepe lifts the characters off the page and into our hearts by allowing us to hear their inner thoughts and feel their emotions. The same storyline in less capable and poetic hands could be cliché. But with Shiepe's gift of subtlety, and a respect for the reader's intelligence, the story is beautiful indeed."

- **JILL FALES**, AUTHOR, *MY LAUNDRY MUSEUM AND OTHER MESSY GIFTS OF MOTHERHOOD*

Cliff Falls

The Missing Pieces Edition

*A novel by* **C.B. Shiepe**

CLIFF FALLS MEDIA | LOS ANGELES, CA

CLIFF FALLS:
THE MISSING PIECES EDITION

BY C.B. SHIEPE

CLIFFFALLS.COM

Cliff   Published by Cliff Falls Media, Inc.
Falls   2275 Huntington Drive, Suite 420, San Marino, CA 91108
Media   OFFICE@CLIFFFALLS.COM

International Standard Book Number – (13): 978-0-9827020-2-4
International Standard Book Number – (10): 0-9827020-2-7
International Standard Book Number – (eBook): 978-0-9827020-3-1
International Standard Book Number – (Audio Book): 978-0-9827020-4-8
Library of Congress Control Number: 2018906211

Printed in the United States of America

New Revised and Expanded Edition, May, 2020

CLIFF FALLS is a trademark registered with the
United States Patent and Trademark Office by Cliff Falls Media, Inc.

Cover design: Sean Teegarden and Jane Moon
Typography: Soo Kim
Author photo: Pam McComb

*This book was written for an audience of One.*

*And is dedicated to my Mom, Marie Anne Shiepe,*
*for her gifts of belief, strength and unconditional love.*

*And to all who struggle, in and out of the spotlight,*
*to know their belovedness.*

"It's one thing to believe in something
when you don't need it to be true.
It's another when everything is riding on it."

— CLAY GRANT

# *A Word Before*

Are you just passing through? I'd say pull up a seat, but the counter is the best place to view all the action at the Acorn Diner. At the counter, you get into great conversations. It's amazing what you learn about people.

We all have a story because we are all recovering from something. If I've learned anything, I've learned that. What you get out of this story probably depends on where you are in your own life right now. If you're in a tough season, you're in good company.

Me? I just stopped in to fill up my thermos with some of the Acorn's "gourmet" coffee. It's a dark roast from Guatemala. Something strong for when you have a long day ahead. My name is Diego and I work up at the church as a groundskeeper. It allows me to live here in Cliff Falls, in these beautiful Santa Cruz Mountains. Anytime I'm away from here, when the city closes in on me, I just think of these mountains and I can breathe again. It's important to breathe, to have those places where you can go and reconnect with yourself and God. I know I need that. But this isn't my story. This is the story of former child star Clay Grant.

If you had told me I could see myself in the life of a former child star, I would have laughed. Most of them are screw-ups, right? But see myself, I did. And it changed me. I don't justify what Clay did—torching a Hollywood studio backlot is never a "good choice"—but when you hear his story you'll understand why he did it and how quickly it got out of control. And why he thought he had no other choice but to run.

They say God speaks in a still small voice, but how can you hear Him if you're never still? Or worse, if other voices speak louder, drowning out your own voice let alone God's? Especially in darker times when you feel like you're suffocating from the world around you?

Clay's struggle is like ours. We all hear voices. The ones we decide to listen to are the ones that matter, that determine how things are going to turn out. Or at least who we are going to become, regardless of how things turn out. But I'm getting ahead of myself.

Now if you've heard another telling, forget it and forgive the author. The other version wasn't a lie. It just wasn't the full truth. Clay had shared so many pieces of himself with the world that it was only natural that he wanted to hold some of the most hurtful pieces back. But the missing pieces make the difference. He's allowed the author to share them now in the hope that they might bring healing to others. I think that's called bravery.

The more we get to know each other, the more comfortable we are sharing our whole story—the light parts and the dark.

The missing pieces that were left out before, well they are now ready to see the light of day.

There are different ways to tell a story. Painting is how I tell mine. So I'll let the author tell you this one. C.B. Shiepe is sitting at the counter right now. The guy in the black V-neck sweater. He's been traveling the country, surprised, but grateful, by the response to Clay's story. Amazed how people from all walks of life connect with it in such a deep, personal way. Maybe we're not so different after all?

See that empty spot at the counter? That's yours. Have a seat and let the author tell you the remarkable journey of Clay Grant.

And remember, Clay was just passing through, too.

~ DIEGO

# Chapter One

*Hollywood Studio Backlot*
*August 16, 1987*

Rising thousands of feet into the air, pillars of heavy smoke could be seen from miles away. It covered the streets filled with fire trucks and police cars. Twenty-three structures lay in ruin. Chicago Alley and Hometown U.S.A. streetscapes were a total loss. The dry rot and plastic sets had burned quickly, the wooden façades igniting like matchboxes. Light from the blaze flickered across the faces of the gathering crowd of overnight studio employees. They watched as the firefighters extinguished the flames on the Hollywood studio backlot.

Wind howling, Burt Cummings sped to the scene in a studio golf cart, praying his instincts weren't true. He dusted embers from the fire off his *Little Guy Mike* black satin jacket that had "Crew" embossed on the front in gold thread. If his gut was right about who started the fire, the studio was going to bury Burt alive in this jacket. His bosses, the moneymakers, would make sure of it. "When I get my hands on *that* kid!"

Burt's golf cart stopped short of the makeshift barricade. Stepping out, the stocky Crewmember searched for the Producer among the firefighters.

Shielding his face from the toxic smoke, Burt ducked under the yellow-black barrier tape. His eyes glared upward at what remained. The rising metal scaffolding was exposed through smoldering chunks of torched foam rubber. It was all that separated the front of the *Little Guy Mike* façade from the back, the outside from the inside. As the smoke cleared, Burt stared into the hollow structure, horrified by the melting tower of *Little Guy Mike* merchandise glowing in the distance— toys, games, and dolls oozing together to form one being. It looked like something out of a Stephen King novel. Its red glow pulsating like a heart struggling to stay alive.

"We found a huge pile of this stuff," a firefighter shouted to the Producer as Burt approached. He held a charred lunch box.

Burt caught the Producer's eye. The day had come.

"It started around back," the firefighter shouted, as he returned to the blaze. "This was no accident."

"You pushed him too hard," the Producer said to Burt. "You gave him no other option."

"You're blaming me?"

"You said he was under control." The Producer tried to contain his rage. "You assured the studio he wasn't a problem."

"I did my job! I did what I needed to do!"

"We paid you to handle him," the Producer said, "not incite him to this." He swept his hand out to encompass the path of destruction.

All Burt saw was everything they had worked for reduced to ashes.

Red embers rained from the sky, but they could have been green from the money that was lost. And not just the physical set, the whole enterprise was destroyed.

"I'm going to kill him!" Burt was an intimidating figure, which, from the studio's perspective, was both a benefit and a curse on set. He was all neck and forearms, having spent equal time at the gym and craft services table. Burt may not have been a real threat to the rest of the world, but to a teenager there was more than a serious power imbalance. "When I get my hands on him!"

"Calm down," the Producer said, attempting to keep Burt in line. "Your short fuse causes more problems than it solves."

"He burned down the lot," Burt said under his breath. He knew that the show and his job were over. Once the public found out who started this, they'd never be able to separate "Little Guy Mike" from the crazed teenager who struck the match. Now Burt was going to be the scapegoat. And worse yet, they'd screw him out of his promised backend deal. The real money they always held out like a carrot on a stick. "I can fix this," Burt said. "I'm going to find him and he'll answer to me!"

"No, you're not. You're finished!"

"Don't blame me!"

The Fire Chief ordered them to move back.

Stepping away, the Producer focused his mind on damage control. "We can still save the syndication." The money was in repeats, mining the show's history. Internationally, they were already being dubbed in Japanese, French, and Italian. The lawyers were now in final negotiations, drawing up contracts. The Producer would have to think quickly to save this ship from sinking. "Let him run."

"What? Look what he did!"

"Clay Grant was never here. Don't you remember? He was with you celebrating his birthday. That is exactly what you're going to say. If you want to get paid." Turning to an enraged Burt, he was adamant, "No one can find out who started this. No one!"

"Don't let him get away with this," Burt fumed.

"Don't worry," the Producer insisted, raising the burnt lunchbox, "he'll pay!"

## Chapter Two

*Earlier that day*

"In just a few moments the Burbank Town Mall welcomes 'Little Guy Mike' on this, his 18th birthday!" The announcer spoke over the loudspeaker.

The crowd roared. The turnout was overwhelming. People filled the expansive central court and upstairs promenade. With excited faces, they chanted his name.

The makeshift backstage was curtained off. Boxes of merchandise were still being carried in by stagehands as a plywood birthday cake was rolled into position. Four feet high, the cake had a hollow back and was decorated on the front with a portrait of a smiling boy wearing a baseball hat and an orange rugby shirt with wide horizontal stripes.

"What do you mean you can't get through the crowd?" Clay shouted into the payphone. He stuffed his leather journal into his back pocket. "I have to be at LAX by 4 p.m. I promised her. I told my mom I'd meet her at the gate!" Removing his baseball hat, he flung it behind some boxes. "I haven't seen my mom in a year!"

The crowd's cheers grew louder.

"I'll get there myself!" Clay hung up the phone. "Nothing is going to spoil this day."

Burt came up behind him, grabbed Clay's journal out of his back pocket and hit him on the head with it, giving him a solid whop. "Where's your hat?"

Burt leaned over Clay, his stocky shadow encompassing him as it always did.

Clay reached for his journal as Burt pushed him away, the force of Burt's forearm keeping Clay at bay. Burt read from it, mocking:

*"All they care about is money. If I died, they'd sell tickets to my funeral. They'd cut a deal with a candy company; stick a few golden tickets in chocolate bars. Even in death they'd find a way to exploit me!"*

"Give it back!" Clay said. He didn't care about money. He never saw it, anyway. All he did fear was selling out, not for the cash, but to please people. And he hated to admit it, but he feared Burt, too.

"Poor little kid." Burt tossed the journal at Clay. "No one cares what you have to say. Why should you? You're an actor, not a writer!"

"And you're a loser!"

Burt made a fist, but there were too many people backstage. "Now where did you hide it?" Burt opened a box searching for the hat. He removed a Halloween mask.

"What the hell is that?" Clay asked, clenching his journal in his hand.

"Looks just like you."

"If I were still eight!" Clay said.

"We got boxes full of this shit," Burt said. "We have to empty the warehouse."

"Get some marshmallows. I'll make a bonfire."

Burt looked at Clay exhausted. "They pay me to make sure the people out there don't know the real you! If they only knew."

Clay ran his fingers through his hair, thinking about the court papers his new lawyer was filing this very day. "Disaffirmance," the right of a new adult at age eighteen to renege on any contract signed on his or her behalf. As part of one contract, Clay's likeness, his very being, was sold for a dollar. Other deals had him working on a summer movie for scale while his managers got a kickback. After an emergency appendectomy, the lawyers even developed an elaborate health plan that drained funds from his so-called protected Coogan account. But the worst deal of all he wouldn't even speak about. During the second season, when cancellation loomed, Clay's mother essentially sold him to his managers for $150,000. Hard to believe but it was true. And he saw it happen to other child stars, performers and athletes. His managers took control of everything. They said it was in Clay's best interest, that they could do more for him than his single mother could, but she should have known better. Mothers are supposed to protect their children, especially if they never had a father. Some give them away because they have to.

Others inflict emotional damage, even physical abuse on their children. But who sells their own son?

Without his mom, Clay learned that the managers created a business framework that trapped him and enriched themselves: a production company, merchandise deals, personal appearance fees, a corrupt legal team... And, worse, everything was court approved. As he discovered, Family Law was clear: "parents of a working child are entitled to its custody, income and service. Children are cattle". And Burt's job was to be the cattle rancher, to ensure their cash cow went moo on cue.

Now Clay was one good judge away from being freed, and the thought filled him with enough hope to try to reconcile with his mom, something he had vowed never to do. But he needed to see her again. Looking into her eyes, he would know: was she tricked or did she do it for the money. And he wanted to believe she was manipulated. Maybe he was being foolish, but that was the power of hope. Despite suffocating from the events around him, this new hope strengthened Clay and put a light back in his eyes. It helped him keep a connection with himself, something only writing in his journal had done. But unlike his journal, this hope told him he had a future, a life beyond all this. This hope even allowed him to stand before the man who had controlled his very breath, to finally stand before his tormentor and not cower. With eyes locked on Burt, Clay couldn't wait for the moment Burt found out the truth. Everything Burt built his life on was about to come to an end.

"One day you'll look and I'll be gone," Clay said quietly but loud enough for Burt to hear.

"You always say that. Where do you think you're going to

go? You're the most famous person in the world," Burt shot back. "Remember, we've got a table set up for you to sign the new product line before we go to the next mall."

"Next mall? I'm not staying!" Clay thought of his mom. He was promised the day off. It would have been his first in five weeks. He spent the last few months touring packed stadiums with that preacher and anti-drug campaign to help bolster his image after the tabloids photographed him smoking a joint. In their eyes, protecting his image was clearly more important than any reality he lived with. Now he just had to get through this event and get to the airport in time to pick up his mom. He kept picturing her waiting, thinking he didn't show up.

"Oh, you're staying. You're signing every last doll, game, and toy in that warehouse!" Burt spotted and then reached for the hat on top of a box. "Put on the hat."

"I'm not wearing—"

Burt grabbed his arm, and shoved the hat on Clay. "Do I need to glue this to your head? No funny business. When you get out there, hit your mark. These kids came to see 'Little Guy Mike' not you!"

Burt let go of his arm.

Clay put his journal back in his pocket, reminding himself that nothing was going to spoil this day. Not even Burt. He took a deep breath, transformed into "Little Guy Mike" and prepared to step onto the stage.

"Oh, by the way, your mom called. She's not coming."

Clay stopped in his tracks, wondering if he heard Burt correctly. "You're lying."

"Some excuse about feeling out of place," Burt said. "Stupid boy. You didn't really think she was going to show, did you?"

Caught between Burt and the crowd, Clay was totally dejected. He couldn't believe he had gotten his hopes up. Was nothing ever going to change?

"See, you can relax now," Burt said. "You don't have to be anywhere but here."

The *Little Guy Mike* theme song started to play as the crowd roared. The mall erupted in song. Everyone could feel the love. Everyone but Clay.

> *One dream short from touching the sky.*
> *Then along came one lit-tle guy.*
> *Now the impossible is just around the bend.*
> *Thanks to our new lit-tle friend.*
> *He's our guy—aye, aye, aye—lit-tle guy.*
> *He's our guy—aye, aye, aye—lit-tle guy. Little Guy Mike!*

"You son of a bitch!" Clay caught Burt's eye. "You did this."

"Burbank, California! Help me welcome 'Little Guy Mike'!" The announcer's voice boomed across the audience. You could feel the mall shake from the excitement.

As usual, there was no time for what Clay was feeling. On cue, he once again transformed himself. Stepping out onto the platform to a cheering crowd, his face was in character. His happy persona was all that held back everything he was feeling inside. But the hurt was stronger.

Defiant, Clay removed his signature baseball hat. The audience roared as he waved it back and forth. Some parents on the second floor looked as if they were prepared to jump. People always wanted a piece of him. They could have it. He tossed it into the crowd, creating pandemonium as the people fought over the hat.

He glanced back at Burt.

This wasn't over.

As Clay walked off the stage, a callous hand grabbed his arm and shook him violently, pinning him up against the wall, his head slamming against the brick. Clay caught his breath in fear, tightening his gut, his shoulder throbbing where it had been dislocated before.

"Not my shoulder!" Clay pleaded.

"What are you going to do, call your lawyer?"

Clay's eyes widened.

"Yes, the bosses know all about your little filing! Are you stupid? They've been planning for this day for years. They won't let their cash cow walk away without a fight!" Twisting his arm tighter, Burt shook it. Clay let out a scream but the cheers from the crowd drowned it out. "The judge will stand by the decision! Everything was court approved and the bosses have plenty of lawyers to make sure it stays that way!" Burt leaned in. "People would kill to have these opportunities. When are you going to grow up? Even your mom doesn't want to be here!"

Burt backed off as a stagehand walked by.

Clay jerked backwards, nursing his shoulder. His eyes filled with hatred.

"Now get to the table! And then get ready for the next mall!"

"No," Clay said defiantly, catching his breath.

With eyes full of rage, Burt turned back, his stocky shadow covering Clay. "What did you say to me?"

# Chapter Three

By the time Clay made it back to the studio, it was already night. He told the stagehand to drop him off just outside the gate. Shoulder throbbing, he wanted to walk the last few blocks. All he felt was disgust and shame. Passing through the gate, he made his way to his trailer to change. The lot was empty. His birthday was almost over.

He closed his eyes and all he saw was Burt.

"I hate *that* man. I hate everyone. Why didn't I just leave?"

Clay had stayed. And signed every doll, game and toy. He took pictures with every kid and every parent who stood in line. And worse yet, he smiled. Like that face plastered on that Halloween mask and on all those toys. Despite everything he was feeling, he smiled. And it made him hate himself. Burt's voice echoed in his head.

*"You didn't really think she was going to show, did you?"*

Fighting off tears, Clay reached under the dash of a nearby studio tram and hotwired it—the igniting of the engine fueling his anger, keeping his tears at bay.

*"You're signing every last doll, game and toy in that warehouse!"*

He sped out of the parking lot, heading straight for the warehouse where they stored the new merchandise, backing up the tram at the receiving dock.

Once inside, he reached for a rope from the warehouse floor and tore open a box marked "LGM Figures", grabbed a "Little Guy Mike" doll and made a knot around its neck.

*"Looks just like you."*

His hurt was stronger than the pain in his shoulder. Box by box Clay filled the tram, determined to have his say. Determined to silence Burt's voice.

*"When you get out there, hit your mark. These kids came to see 'Little Guy Mike' not you!"*

Overflowing with *Little Guy Mike* merchandise, Clay pulled the tram out of the parking lot and raced down the historic back lot. Winding through the façade-lined streets, he accelerated past the timber-framed structures, the famed sets from television and motion pictures. It was as if the façades were calling out to him, pleading for him to turn back. But he wouldn't listen. Finally, the tram stopped, a LGM doll with a noose around its neck dangling from the rear view mirror.

Stepping off the tram, Clay gathered as much as he could carry and approached the *Little Guy Mike* set. Season after season, this façade was the symbol of the typical American home life. The happy existence the show perpetuated, but something that he never knew.

The house itself was idyllic, but hollow. The white clapboard sparkled like freshly polished teeth. Empty pillars only appeared to support the stylized arch made of plywood and rubber. The yard was well manicured, though closer inspection revealed plastic flowers and trees propped up by wooden braces.

Over the years, the exterior had been painted many times, its red shutters and foam clapboard well maintained. But the inside remained the same—like him, a dusty dumping ground of empty paint cans and discarded props. It was messy and murky, a place not created for the camera.

With arms filled, he carried the contents through the bright red door with polished brass knocker, to the outside patch of dirt on the other side of the façade. Back and forth he went, tirelessly piling item upon item. As much as he tried he was still unable to discern Burt's voice from his own.

*"No one cares what you have to say. Why should you?"*

The tram nearly emptied, Clay reached for the last box, a "Little Guy Mike" Halloween costume, the cardboard perimeter decorated with playful images of the character. He stared at the plastic mask suffocating beneath the thin layer of cellophane. Taking it out, Clay held it up against the night sky, the moonlight illuminating its cutout eyes.

*"Looks just like you."*

The contoured face with rouge cheeks was anything but natural; the forced expression of a mischievous child was haunting. He hated this mask.

Clay placed the plastic mask face up, on top of the great mound of *Little Guy Mike* merchandise. Then he struck a match.

The smiling mask slowly melted as the flames spread. Toxic fumes filled the air.

Clay's youthful face basked in the orange glow of the blaze, his green eyes staring blankly into the fire. He reached into his back pocket and retrieved his journal. Maybe he should let that burn too? He held it over the flames, the smell of burnt leather as the spine singed.

*"No one cares what you have to say. Why should you?"*

It was hopeless. His voice couldn't silence Burt's voice. He was done. He had nothing left to say, which was why he was surprised when the words came:

*...scared children—all of us—dealing with adult things— wondering if we are that strong. And everyone wants us to be someone or something else.*

Consumed with this truth, he pulled his hand back. Clutching the journal, he ascended the scaffolding of the façade, climbing above the melting tower of products and silvery streams of smoke.

Clay settled into his usual spot.

*Chapter Four*

Perched above the studio backlot, above the hanging cables and darkened floodlights, Clay scribbled away under the star-filled sky as his pathetic fire died out below. His acid-washed jeans and faded U2 T-shirt under a nylon jacket were his only shield from the night wind. But he didn't care.

It was not unusual for him to return after dark, ascend the rusty scaffolding, and sometimes after a long wait find refuge in the unexpected words that came to him, but this night was different. He didn't have to wait for the words to come; they arrived on their own. They poured out. Out of his being. Out of his heart. Out of his pen, howling like the intensifying Santa Ana winds that swept against his face, that ruffled his dyed black hair.

With ink-stained fingers, he wrote it all down. Every word. Just as he heard it, he wrote it down.

*"...scared children—all of us—dealing with adult things—*

wondering if we are that strong. And everyone wants
us to be someone or something else."

Tears streaming down his face, Clay was somehow
comforted as he listened. This voice was different from Burt's
and it connected him with his own.

"The voice knows how I feel. It always does. How
it feels to be bullied. How it feels when people use
you, when they think they own you! How it feels
when your every screw-up is captured on camera or
in print. How it feels when there's a self out there
being marketed that isn't you!

"I tell myself that I don't care about anyone or
anything, but I do care. I hate that. Why can't I
shut that part of myself down?"

Leaning back against the crude pipes that supported the
structure, his legs dangled off the plywood ledge. This was
the backside of the façade, the ugly side. His refuge. Burt—
that asshole—was right. Clay didn't have anywhere to go. All
this fame and the only spot where he could find an ounce of
peace was behind this façade. He steadied the flapping pages
in his journal as he wrote. He wrote about every fear, every
expectation, what his life was *really* like, as the one phrase
repeated in his spirit.

...*scared children—all of us—dealing with adult things—
wondering if we are that strong. And everyone wants us to be
someone or something else.*

His green eyes glanced up from the page and looked below.

The smoldering fire was nearly out. What did I do? Waves of embarrassment and shame overwhelmed him. He thought about the parents on the second floor of the mall who almost jumped when he tossed the hat into the crowd.

"The world envies me, but I would trade shoes in a heartbeat with any of the kids outside the gate. Growing up on the lot, I could see them in the park across the street playing with their parents and I wished my days were as ordinary as that. I've never known the difference between a normal childhood and this."

He closed his eyes and the image of his mother came to him. Was I ever just a kid?

"My earliest memories are of going on auditions with you, working commercials and print ads after winning that contest in our hometown. I'm still waiting for my pinchable cheeks to lean out. It was fun back then and we would always go for ice cream afterwards. That was the last time I felt normal."

Gripping the pen, Clay knew he was always trying to get back to that place of feeling normal.

"Since I was 12, you haven't been in the picture, except for when the show was on hiatus or during a few visits throughout the year. Who does that?

*"I will never forgive you for leaving me with them.
Never!!!"*

Clay's tears dripped onto the page, smudging the ink.
He had believed that things would get better; that things
would change even though everything around him told him
differently. He only gave his mom another chance after she
promised that she would be there for him.

*"I'm an idiot. I can't believe that after how much
you hurt me, I was looking forward to you showing
up! You'd think I'd be over all this. But I just feel
the same!*

*"I'm sick of this life! I'm sick of all the things I
have to care about! The audience. The ratings. The
advertisers. Studio executives. My image. Everyone
else's feelings! Everyone else's expectations! Screw
them all!!! I don't want to care about anyone else but
me!!! Besides, they're never happy.*

*"All I know is that I have this desire to have control,
to get it all back. All those pieces of myself that
were sold, rented, stolen, or squashed. To take back
every false perception of who they say I am. Dear
God. Just for a day I want the inside and the
outside to be the same."*

Lost in his thoughts, Clay barely noticed that the night
wind had become more pronounced, like the words streaming

out of his soul. The Santa Ana was invigorating, and like all things that made him feel alive, it was also dangerous. A danger he didn't realize until it was too late, until the reignited embers filled the air and dusted the pages of his journal.

The gale-force winds shook the structure, his leather journal slipping from his grasp and falling into the blaze. Gripping the jagged beams as he climbed down the scaffolding, he removed his jacket and beat it hopelessly against the emboldened flames. But they continued to mount, crawling up the side of the façade, rising like shameful prayers finally released.

Spotting his journal, Clay wrapped his hand in his jacket and reached into the flames to retrieve it.

He froze for what seemed an eternity as he realized that the fire was out of control. Smoke surrounded him, engulfing the scaffolding and dimming the star-filled sky. After making his way through the front door, Clay turned back, his glossy eyes taking one last look at the show's set. The façade was rapidly turning black, the entire structure was on fire, and worse, it was spreading.

As the backlot burned, he made his choice. Clenching his journal, Clay Grant ran into the night and disappeared into the thick smoke.

# Chapter Five

*Fifteen years after the fire*
*May 6, 2002*

"Sometimes a picture is worth more than a thousand words," the photographer thought. He removed the extended lens from his Minolta. Placing it securely in the camera bag, he glanced briefly across the room at *Entertainment Now* airing on the Colorado motel television set. It was the weekend edition hosted by Kat Stone.

*"Fifteen years on the run. He was America's guy as the star of the 80's sitcom hit Little Guy Mike, about the antics of a lovable orphan. Then he vanished the same night a mysterious fire burned down the studio's historic backlot. Whatever happened to Clay Grant?"*

The man tossed the empty suitcase onto the mattress and opened it.

Nauseous from the altitude, he sat down momentarily on the side of the bed. His eyes returned to the television.

*"Although an official studio investigation did not link Clay Grant to the fire, he disappeared from the public eye and later from Uncle Sam, reportedly owing the IRS more than four hundred thousand dollars in back taxes."*

Standing up, the man started packing. He was confident that interest in Clay had not faded in the years since the fire. There was still a market for the former child star and this photographer was betting on it. He tossed his toiletries into the suitcase, along with two towels from the motel bathroom.

*"It seems everyone is looking for this missing star on the run. In this ENZ exclusive, our reporters tracked down Clay's last hiding place in Beaver Creek, Colorado and spoke with his former landlady."*

The photographer stopped packing, went to the television and turned up the volume. Crouching down, his attention was glued to the screen. He didn't intend to be on television, and was surprised the crew had captured him taking pictures in the distance.

Gripping the remote, Burt Cummings recognized himself in the shot, right in the middle of the reporter and landlady in her terrycloth bathrobe. There he was, camera flashing in the background, like an eager extra attracting more attention than the principal. Show off. Despite an additional twenty pounds, he thought he looked good on television. Not bad for fifty-two. He was quick to ignore the thinning hair and wide forehead that merged into a scalp. At one time he had harbored thoughts of having a career. He would have made a good character actor, "the heavy" in gangster films, he thought.

But that was before he decided to go behind the camera.

Burt had only been a Crewmember a year when he started working for the managers who were trying to buy Clay. He helped convince Clay's mother to sell him to the team and stood to profit considerably. Yes, he got kickbacks for keeping Clay in line, but the real money was to come later. Sometimes his methods were heavy-handed, but "the brat" was impossible to control, especially as he got older. Burt never did work again. He was blacklisted. The studio blamed him for provoking the kid. After all that sweat equity, he lost his reputation and his promised share of the backend earnings. Merchandise cut. Gone. Production deal. Gone. Personal appearance fee. Gone. Clay! Gone! Gone! Gone! Despite his side deal, he never got a cut of that money. Everything was leveraged and everything was lost. Had Burt known how it would play out, he would have tracked Clay down that night and made him pay on his own.

Burt pulled out his wallet and removed a tattered photo. It was of Clay, maybe twelve years old. This had always been his secret weapon, his ultimate leverage. Every time he looked at it he was reminded that Clay was vulnerable, weak, nothing like what the world saw. He was stripped of all the adulation, reduced to what Burt saw him as, someone he could control. Burt may have not owned Clay like the managers, but there were other ways of owning a person.

Standing up quickly, he leaned against the television stand, again feeling the effects from the altitude. He shut his eyes as the reporter continued interviewing the landlady.

*"I didn't know who he was, but he owes me three months' rent."*

*"Do you have any indication where he went?"* the reporter asked, pressing his microphone up to her face.

*"He owes me three months' rent!"*

Burt slammed the suitcase shut. He didn't know where Clay was, but he knew where he could find out. And she was going to tell him. Or else. He left the motel room without bothering to turn off the television.

*"Missing in action and outrunning the IRS. So where is 'Little Guy Mike'?"*

## Chapter Six

*August 16, 2002*

Clay opened his eyes from a perfect night's sleep. The deep green eyes were the same, but the boy had faded, at least on the outside. He was thirty-three. His face masculine, his cheekbones and jaw defined. His hair, once perpetually dyed black by the powers that be, was now his natural unruly chestnut brown and covered his eyes when he sneezed. He looked so different that on occasion when people would tell him he resembled LGM, he'd just laugh and say, "That fool?"

Looking different was one way to separate the present from the past; that and making sure he was constantly moving. He always kept his knit hat in his back pocket and a duffel bag packed with a few essentials, just in case.

Squinting against the persistent gleam of light coming through the pane-glassed window, Clay smelled seawater from the rugged harbor. "Room with a view" the ad read. It was the only window in the frugal saltbox. Set back, deep within the thick colonial wall, it was more like a porthole. He repositioned his head in the pillow. Hey, it's a view.

He had been in Charlestown, Massachusetts three months, almost the whole summer. At least I'm sleeping through the night. For that he was grateful. It always took him this long to settle into a new town. And just when he would start to feel at home, something would happen that would force him to move on.

He would still be in Beaver Creek, Colorado had that ski instructor not recognized him. Did I have to ask out a former president of my fan club?

This was always his dilemma: contort yourself to please others or stay true to yourself and be alone. For the past fifteen years, he chose the latter.

As a result, he had no one to talk to. Really talk to. Writing was his only solace and now he was not even doing that. Words only made him more aware of what he could never change. And the voice that always comforted him, the one that he used to hear on the scaffolding, was now distant and faint. Why bother?

Nestling his head in the pillow, he cherished these moments in bed, hidden beneath the protective summer blanket, and his feet tucked into the soft cotton sheet secured to the mattress.

I could spend eternity in here. Okay, so a coffin offers the same benefits.

Clay felt that burnt leather journal tucked under his mattress. The irony of sleeping atop his buried feelings. He never had the heart to throw it away and still he couldn't open it. If there were a day to open it, it would be today, his birthday. But he knew better. He couldn't risk being consumed by the memories.

Drifting back to sleep, the question every year was the same. Do I really have to sing to myself?

Every year on his birthday, he did his best not to think about the night of the fire or the days that followed when he found himself in Costa Rica trying to disappear. Most runaways went to Hollywood. Clay ran everywhere else. South America, Thailand, and then Europe, backpacking until the money ran out. It was nearly three years before he realized the studio covered up his involvement in the fire. He couldn't figure out why until he started seeing his face pop up on billboards and newsstands across Europe. The syndication was growing year by year. It didn't matter how obscure the town was.

He was in the Black Forest when he first learned about his troubles with the IRS. Clay didn't need to read German to know he wasn't responsible for a tax debt when he never saw a profit. Obviously, this was payback for covering up the fire.

Every place he went, *Little Guy Mike* followed. When he saw a child wearing a "Little Guy Mike" Halloween mask during Carnival, he knew it was time to go back. He was homesick and because of the syndication, *Little Guy Mike* was more popular abroad than it had been in the States. That was five years ago.

He had been to so many places, but because he kept to himself, each place felt the same.

Yawning, he peeked at the blurry red numbers on the alarm clock, 5:27 a.m.

"Crap!"

Jumping from bed as if an army officer had entered the barracks, Clay stumbled over his duffel bag in the dark. He tumbled backwards onto the knotted pine floor. He seldom landed on his feet, but he did land.

Flat on his back, Clay stared upward. The low ceiling, like Heaven, always seemed higher from this vantage point. He pulled himself up, which he was also accustomed to doing.

"I'm getting too old for this."

As he rose, he saw her. This had become a morning ritual. Through that porthole of a window, he stared at her. The flapping colorful flags were draped over her elaborate rigging. The crew climbed her three proud masts, lowering her vast sails. Whatever majestic was, she was it. U.S.S. Constitution. Old Ironsides. She made him want to be a better man. That inspiration was hard to come by.

The heartless clock showed 5:31 a.m. "Crap!"

\*

Boston is a walking town, but Clay was running.

Since the night of the fire, he never had a good feeling about his birthday. And why would he? He always felt something bad was going to happen. Usually it did.

The North Washington Street Bridge connected Charlestown to the North End, crossing Boston Harbor where it met the Charles River. Sprinting across in record time, his frantic pace conjured up memories of being late to set. An unforgiving crew could make life miserable for a kid. It didn't matter that Clay was the star. The cold shoulder lasted weeks. It was never his intention to be late. It was just his nature.

Traveling along the Freedom Trail, his swift feet followed the red brick line, darting past historical markers. Churches. Meetinghouses. Burial grounds. They told the story of Boston's and the nation's struggle for freedom.

Clay appreciated that liberty was a precious thing and worth fighting for. But he wasn't interested in retracing his own Freedom Trail, that uneven road that began the night of the fire. As far as he was concerned, the people and events of his past were all best left in the past. He had paid a heavy price for running away and did everything in his power to ensure that it wasn't in vain.

With each stride, Clay was always one wrong step away from his face being plastered on every television network around the globe or having another ghost from his past being unearthed. One in particular who was relentlessly cruel.

Quickening his pace, Clay glanced up to align himself with the Old North Church's towering steeple. It was a constant beacon to ships entering the harbor. His on-set tutor had made sure he knew the history.

Sometime before midnight, in 1770-something, Randy Newman...no, Robert Newman climbed the darkened belfry and held high two lanterns. It was a sign from Paul Revere that the British were coming! And by sea, not land. That event ignited the American Revolution. Clay only wished that he had such warnings.

He'd like to think that God would give him a sign of impending danger but he knew better than to get his hopes up. Been there. Done that. Still something deep in his heart wanted to believe that God was looking out for him.

He looked at that belfry as he raced by. If warning lanterns were left for Clay on this day, he couldn't tell as the rapidly emerging sun shined in his eyes and obscured his sight.

The Italian North End was already awake. Street vendors scattered empty produce crates among the stalls opening for the day. Merchants arranged fresh fish in open containers filled with ice, while grandmothers hung laundry off tenement balconies.

Racing through the narrow walkways and alleys, Clay darted under a grand banner strung across the street.

## 91ST ANNUAL
## FISHERMAN'S FEAST & ANGEL FLIGHT
August 15th—18th
Music, Food and Fireworks!

It had been a summer of feasts and this would be the largest. Clay avoided crowds, reminding himself that a quiet existence would be possible once Labor Day passed. That is, if he still had a job.

He got paid today. After taking care of a few expenses, he knew he would finally have enough cash to send to his former landlady in Colorado.

Catching his breath, he arrived at 300 Hanover Street. The brown marquee announced "Mike's Pastry" in stylized yellow lettering. It was a fixture in the immigrant neighborhood for more than fifty years and attracted regular customers as well as tourists. It had occurred to him that "Little Guy Mike" working at Mike's Pastry was the equivalent of hiding in plain sight. So far, the strategy had worked.

Clay went around back and cautiously poked his head in the door. His best bet was to slip in once the manager was out of sight.

If Santa were Italian, this was what his workshop would look like. Specialty cakes spinning on wheels as bakers added decorations. Trays of macaroons being removed from the stainless steel ovens. Eggs added to dough churning in the industrial mixer. The aroma was invigorating. He loved this place.

The bakers were loading pastry bags with ricotta cheese. They took a golden cannoli shell in one hand and filled each side before dipping the ends in chocolate chips or pistachios, dusting the top with confectioner's sugar.

Clay caught the eye of one of the bakers.

"Coast is clear," the baker said. "He's in the front."

Stepping into the kitchen, Clay was careful to avoid Angelo De Spirito, the bakery's manager. "You guys are the best," he spoke softly. And they were. In the past three months he had yet to endure the cold shoulder. They didn't know who he was, but his quirky ways were a welcome distraction, as were his stories of Italy. As Clay was greeted by a host of first generation Italian bakers, he spotted Angelo approaching.

A baker intercepted Angelo by rolling a six-foot rack of cannoli shells in front of Clay. Another slid an apron over Clay's head, before the first baker spun the rack around. The guys always looked out for Clay. However, when Clay turned around he was face to face with Angelo.

"Again late," the stout manager reprimanded. "Everyone else 4:30. You 6:10!"

Clay nodded in agreement. He knew silence was his best bet.

"If the feast didn't start tonight!"

Clay continued to nod.

"Get to work!"

Smiling, Clay got to work, moving the rack filled with cannoli. As soon as Angelo turned his back, he sneaked one. Tasted as good as it looked. Not a bad breakfast. Happy Birthday to me.

Wiping the cream from his mouth, his heart allowed him to say something unexpected, "Nothing is going to spoil this day."

Just as the words rolled off his lips, a furious Angelo stepped in front of him.

# Chapter Seven

The North End readied for the feast. People assembled carnival games. Policemen sectioned off streets. Workers erected a stage in the square. Volunteers on ladders attached green, white and red decorations to the lampposts.

At Mike's Pastry a line stretched out the door despite the hot and humid August weather. Among those toward the back of the line was a stocky man with a Minolta slung over his shoulder. Excitement raced through his body. Casing his surroundings, Burt attempted to blend in with everyone else in line, while still trying to keep everyone at a distance. Patience was not one of his virtues. But if the address was right, he wasn't about to blow the element of surprise. Some might call Burt a stalker, but he knew he had every right to make Clay pay. And he had played out this moment in his head a million times before.

Inside, the bakery was packed, bustling with a mixture of tourists and locals pressing up against the enormous glass case overflowing with authentic Italian pastry. Everything in this place was the real thing. Pistachio macaroons. Almond biscotti. Chocolate Florentines. Lemon rings. Rainbow cookies. Apricot bows. Napoleons. Fig squares. Tiramisu.

"Two pounds of the white cherry macaroons!" one lady shouted, pointing to the glass case. "And a Lobster tail! With chocolate cream!"

The activity was chaotic. Numbers were yelled out as workers anxiously filled boxes, before wrapping them with white-and-blue string.

In the kitchen, the bakers intensified the pace, attempting to keep up with the demand. But Clay was out back, assigned to a "special project" in the alley.

Clay unloaded bags of flour from the delivery truck, stopping momentarily to wipe the sweat from his forehead. The heat was oppressive, and he was obviously not happy.

"Next time, on time," Angelo gloated.

Clay offered a tortured stare, convinced Angelo was a studio boss in a former life. He hurled another bag off the truck.

As soon as Angelo returned to the kitchen, Bella, the manager's ten-year-old daughter, appeared from behind the delivery truck. Bella wore jean shorts and a pink Red Sox jersey. Her naturally curly hair framed a cherub face that lit up when she smiled. So much personality in such a little body, Bella was exactly the type of kid sitcoms were built around. Clay was grateful a Hollywood scout hadn't discovered her yet, but he knew with the feast starting tonight that it just might be a matter of time.

"This will cool you off," Bella said. She held two Italian ices, one in each hand.

"Lemon?" Clay shouted from the truck.

"Of course!"

Clay leaped off the truck overjoyed. Lemon was his favorite. Stumbling as he made his landing, he regained his balance just in time to avoid falling to the ground.

Exhaling, Bella handed him his Italian ice.

"You really are an angel," Clay said. Wiping his brow, he held the cold cup against his face. "I can see why they picked you over all the other girls."

"But I don't want to be the angel!" Bella said, brushing her curly locks from her face.

"Why?"

"The girl who's the angel has to hang from that!" Bella pointed to a rope and pulley across the street. It was three stories up, higher than the banner announcing the feast. "That's high!"

Wouldn't catch me up there, Clay thought to himself.

"And with all those people staring at me, I won't be able to remember the prayer!"

Squeezing the last of his ice from the white paper cup, he realized that Bella hadn't touched hers.

"They keep saying I'm lucky. Lucky! But I don't want to do it!" She sat down discouraged, handing Clay her ice.

Clay always did his best to numb his gift of empathy. Although it was the same quality that made him a good actor, it was a dangerous can of worms to open. It made him feel too deeply, sometimes for people who didn't deserve it. But what this little girl was feeling hit too close to home.

The Italian ice in Clay's hand dissolved under the hot sun,

but he didn't notice. Realizing how afraid she was, he turned his attention to the rope and pulley, envisioning her dangling above the crowded streets, the people cheering, shouting her name. He knew how overwhelming it could be: the noise, the lights. And the panic that could set in.

In that moment, everything disappeared. Clay was on set again, just a boy in that stupid dream sequence space suit, dangling above the studio audience.

*Blinded by the spotlights, he was hanging there with that ridiculous fishbowl helmet over his head, struggling to breathe, terrified that the wires couldn't hold him. The theme song filled the studio, the crowd screaming his name.*

*"Where's my mom?" the boy shouted, gasping for air. Searching the crowd of unfamiliar faces below, she was nowhere to be found.*

*"Somebody! Anybody!" He was certain the wires would snap, the crowd below ready to consume him.*

*"Help me!" His desperate cries fell on deaf ears. He realized that he wasn't mic'ed!*

*Clay looked to the heavens. "Get me down!" the boy yelled, his breath fogging up the plastic helmet. "Get me down!"*

Bella tugged on his shirt. "What is it?"

Clay came to himself, realizing that Bella was beside him. "You shouldn't have to do it if you don't want to. That's what I think. You're a little girl, not the entertainment!"

"But I don't have a choice! What can I do?"

"Maybe you can talk to your dad?"

"He'll kill me!"

Bella didn't have a choice, and nobody understood that better than Clay. Everything inside of him wanted to tell her the truth—that there was nothing she could do, but he didn't want to crush her spirit.

Placing her hands on the sides of her face, she stared hopelessly at the cobblestone pavement. "I'm scared! What can I do?"

If there was a time to be profound, this was it. At a loss for words, Clay considered what he would do. He was grateful for time to think while a noisy delivery truck passed by them in the alley.

"If it were me, I'd tell myself I didn't choose this," Clay said.

"I didn't choose this!" Bella said, throwing her hands in the air, agreeing.

"But I'm up here," Clay said. He jumped on the bags of flour to emphasize the point. "So..."

Bella raised her head in expectation. "So?"

"So..." Clay pointed at the pulley and rope, completing his thought. "I might as well fly!"

"That's all you got?" Bella shouted.

Clay jumped off the stack of bags. "That's all I got."

The little girl was distraught. Tears streaming down her face, Bella cried, twirling her curly locks with her finger. "I don't want to do it!"

"Hey, don't worry. You're not going to be alone. I'm going to be there. If you don't like it, I'll make them bring you right down."

"What if they won't?"

"See that building across the way. If you want I can be on the rooftop so when they hoist you up, you'll be eye level with me—just like we are now. You keep looking at me and it will be just like you're on the ground."

"You promise?"

Clay crossed his heart. "I promise."

Unexpectedly, Angelo appeared from the kitchen, catching the two speaking. "No breaks! No breaks!"

Clay grabbed a sack of flour in an attempt to look busy, but Angelo was focused on Bella.

"Go learn your prayer!" Angelo hollered.

Determined to get out of this honor, Bella abruptly stood up and confronted her father. "I don't want to do it!"

"What you mean?" her father said, towering over her.

Bella recognized her height disadvantage. Mustering up her courage, she climbed on top of the bags of flour and was now eye level with her father.

"I'm a little girl, not the entertainment!" she declared, pointing at the pulley and rope.

Angelo looked angrily at Clay who looked away.

"I'm serious, Papa. I'm not doing it."

Angelo slowly leaned forward, and then fumed, "Go! Learn your prayer!"

Bella jumped off the stack and ran off discouraged.

Angelo turned to Clay. "You're fired!"

Inside the crowded bakery, Burt pushed his way to the front of the line. Pressed up against the glass case, Burt caught the attention of one of the ladies behind the counter. "Over here!"

"You need to take a number," she fired back.

"I'm looking for somebody. An old friend." As the woman leaned over the counter, Burt spoke into her ear, describing

Clay. The lady pointed out back.

Adrenaline raced through his body. After all this time, the kid who ruined his life was now in range. Payback time! Excited, Burt attempted to push his way through the crowd, but it was too thick. There was no way he was going to blow this chance. Peeking into the kitchen he spotted the screen door and opted for the more direct path.

To the amazement of all in the bakery, Burt ducked under the counter. Running into the kitchen, he raced past the bakers who swung their trays of cannoli out of his way, and then he rushed out the back door into the alley.

Clay untied his apron and was pulling it over his head when he looked up and spotted Burt. Their eyes locked on each other. Fifteen years to the day.

"No!!!" Clay shouted, shocked to see Burt again.

Readying his camera, Burt charged at him. "Happy Birthday!"

Desperate, Clay reached for a bag of flour and, using all his weight, hurled it at Burt. As the bag made contact, Clay fell forward as the seams split open. Both Clay and Burt crashed to the ground as a massive cloud of flour erupted followed by the bright flash of the camera.

# Chapter Eight

*Stanford University Hospital*

*"Fact or Fake? Is this really Clay Grant, the elusive sitcom star seldom seen as an adult? 'Could be,' says one ENZ source that reports assault charges have been filed in Boston against this outlaw on the run."*

If there were a name Ted Mitchell never needed to hear again, it was Clay Grant. But like an accident on the freeway, he couldn't divert his eyes.

Ted walked toward the television in the hospital lobby, fixated on the photograph. It was of a guy amidst a cloud of flour. Only his eyes were partially visible. Is that him?

*"Over the years, there have been thousands of 'Little Guy Mike' sightings. The only problem is no one knows what Clay Grant looks like now."*

Ted leaned in.

*"Here is one of his last public appearances at the Orange Bowl*

*in Miami."*

Clay was joined on stage by inspirational pastor Reagan Mitchell and his teenage son.

Ted watched a younger version of himself standing beside his father. It had been years since he had seen the clip. They had spent the summer touring stadiums with that anti-drug campaign and were halfway through when Clay was added to the line-up to help improve his public image after being caught smoking pot. While Ted and his family actually cared about the message they shared, all too often Clay had been inches away from undermining everything. Thinking of it now still irked Ted.

*"Boys, what do you do when someone asks you to take drugs?"* Pastor Reagan Mitchell asked.

Clay and Ted shouted, *"Just say no!"*

Smirking, Ted was surprised Clay had stayed under the radar this long. A guy like that creates trouble wherever he goes. In Ted's opinion, Clay was everything Ted was not: reckless, impulsive and never concerned with making the right choice. The son of the pastor and always under the church's watchful eye, Ted struggled to make straight A's and maintain his position on the varsity track team. He expected that good things came to those who worked hard for them. At least that's what he had been taught. But as life went by, it seemed to be telling him something different, especially now. He didn't want to admit it, but Ted secretly envied Clay's ability to get up and run at the first sign of trouble. He only wished he was capable of doing the same.

Moving down the hall, Ted continued his quest for Stanford University Hospital's late night version of dinner. So far he had mistakenly discovered the pharmacy, psychiatric ward, and even the morgue, but no vending machine. Dollar bill in hand, he was unwilling to admit that he might have been sent on a wild goose chase.

Just when he was about to give up, he turned the corner and spotted the machine inside a newly remodeled waiting room he had not yet discovered. This area was quieter than the one he had been sleeping in and boasted a new flat screen television.

Through the vending machine's glass, Ted searched for something healthy among the processed, fried, sugary, fat-filled choices. His options were limited. Apple fruit pie. BBQ potato chips. Raspberry butter cookies. Gummy bears. Marshmallow-rice treat. Cheese puffs. Despite being sleep deprived, he wasn't giving in yet. A granola bar. There we go.

Ted was fit and always tried to make the right choice when it came to eating and to life. This was his unspoken deal with God: choose wisely and nothing bad will happen.

Feeding his dollar into the machine, it promptly spit it out. Ted flattened the dollar with his thumbs and fed it again. Rejected! Ted was annoyed, but determined. Rubbing the dollar against the edge of the machine, he fed it once more. Success! Pressing E4 on the touchpad, Ted watched as the coil started to turn. Come on. Come on. The granola bar inched forward, the coil continuing its counter-clockwise rotation. His stomach growled. Come on!

Then, before his widened eyes, the coil jammed, lodging the granola bar and leaving it dangling in midair. Another right choice ending in frustration. Everything inside of Ted wanted to kick that machine, but as usual, he showed restraint.

He tapped the glass a few times, but the granola bar wouldn't budge. He tapped it harder. No luck. Ted looked to his right and to his left to make sure he was alone. Then, placing his hands on each side of that machine, Ted shook it violently. Huffing and puffing, he stared into the glass, trying to make his good choice payoff, but nothing happened.

"You need to push it from the front."

Ted looked over his shoulder. Tyler, his nine-year-old son, was standing beside him.

"I'm supposed to tell you that Mom called *again* and that Grandpa wants Doritos."

"Tell Grandpa the vending machine is broken," Ted said calmly, arms hugging the contraption. "And that I'll see him back in the room."

As Tyler walked away, Ted banged his head in defeat against the glass. The granola bar dislodged from the coil, falling within reach. Ted looked at his own reflection. Idiot.

Retrieving the bar, he tore the wrapper open and began chewing his hard-fought prize. Ted crumpled the wrapper and looked for a trashcan. Not spotting one, he reluctantly put the wrapper into his pocket before turning and walking away.

*

Rose Mitchell's eyes transcended everything. The sterile hospital room. The sickness. Her failing body. Her husband, Reagan, could not imagine that that light would ever go out. He gently wiped her forehead with a moist cloth as the nurse administered the medication intravenously, the drops of fluid working their way into her system to offset the waves of pain and nausea. Skirting her brow with the cloth, he watched as she stared into the distance.

Before he could look away, Rose caught him. She looked right at him, attuned to his introspection and bothered by the special attention. "I'm not afraid. When God wants me, He wants me."

"Well, right now we want you." Reagan wasn't one to concede a challenge, even one that had long been decided. She'd been given six months. That was eight months ago. He resumed wiping her brow, discreetly glancing at the nurse.

"She should be feeling this soon," the nurse assured him.

Rose rolled her tired eyes. She couldn't understand it. Death was a part of life. To her it was a natural progression, one that she had made peace with long ago.

"Death isn't scary, living is," Rose said, scolding Reagan and the nurse, "Nobody can escape it."

"Death and taxes," Reagan said, conferring with the nurse.

Rose corrected them. "Life. Nobody escapes life."

Reagan knew Rose was right. She usually was. Her weakness only made that strength more apparent.

Rose reached out and touched his hand. "You're holding him back. Ted will never be a man until you let him fail and learn to pick himself up."

Reagan would do anything for her, but this was one request that put everything they had built in jeopardy.

"Don't you worry about any of that now—"

"The one I'm worried about is you. When I'm gone who is going to comfort the 'Comforter in Chief'?"

Resting her eyes, the medication took effect. "Nobody escapes life."

Reagan watched as she began to drift. He wanted to escape everything that he knew was coming. If he were honest, that's what he wanted to do. But he wasn't going to leave Rose. She was his girl and the one who always held him together. She was his North.

Reagan knew how to be a visionary and he knew how to help people, but this he didn't know how to deal with. The idea that she was slipping from his grasp made him feel powerless, and he hated that. And it made him want to run.

"That's you!" the nurse said, pointing to the television and reaching for the volume control. "You and your son!"

Reagan looked up, recognizing himself on the TV. He had not seen the footage in years.

*"Here is one of his last public appearances at the Orange Bowl in Miami."*

Reagan, Clay and Ted stood on the stage together.

*"Boys, what do you do when someone asks you to take drugs?"*

Clay and Ted shouted, *"Just say no!"*

"Another child star. Another mess," the nurse said. "I'll go find your son and tell him he's on television." The nurse left the room.

"What is it?" Rose said, opening her eyes.

"They found him. Clay. After all these years."

A blurry photo of Clay covered in flour appeared on screen. Only his eyes were visible.

*"Fifteen years after the mysterious fire, have we finally found 'Little Guy Mike'? We have an insider in Boston investigating the assault charges to confirm whether this is real or just another Clay Grant rumor."*

Rose looked at Reagan, shaking her head. He knew

that look.

"Maybe it's not him?" Reagan reasoned, sensing Rose's concern. He didn't want her to get upset.

"I know those eyes." She pointed to the screen, fighting off the effects of the medication. "It's not human how they continue to exploit that child. We should have done something. Some adult should have done something."

"I've often thought that, but I still don't know what we could have done."

"That night I found him. Something ugly had happened—something violent—but he wouldn't let me in. He was writing all night. It was so..." Rose's voice cracked.

"I know," Reagan said, patting her arm.

Rose struggled to stay awake. "If I was able, I would fly there and help the boy myself."

"I believe you would," Reagan said. "I believe you would."

A few hours later, Reagan took the elevator down to the lobby. As the last rays of sun faded from the sky, he exited the hospital, distraught. He couldn't mask his pain. He looked to his right and left, paranoid that others could tell what he was feeling inside. He felt the people all around him, closing in. He pulled out his cell phone.

"I need a plane ticket."

# Chapter Nine

Through the iron-barred window, sounds from the first night of the feast filled the Old North End Jail. Fireworks bursting. Accordions humming. People cheering.

Still covered in flour, Clay sat defeated on the cell's cold cement floor. He couldn't figure it out. How does Burt keep finding me?

Pressing his hands against his ears, Clay leaned back against the crude brick wall. He hated the sound of a massive crowd, that imposing mixture of screams and laughter that violated his being. All he ever wanted was not to feel this again.

Over the years, Clay had always managed to stay one step ahead of Burt. But that was getting increasingly harder to do. Seeing Burt today, even for only that moment, unleashed a flood of his constant accusations. They were louder than the sounds coming from outside the cell. And they were louder than Clay's own voice, let alone God's voice.

*"You fatherless bastard. Look around. It's always your fault!*

*Bad seed. Even your mom doesn't want to be with you. If people only knew the real you!"*

Clay wanted to get up and run away, needing to make the feelings dissipate. But he was trapped.

Here he was helpless again. His tormentor was within range.

Looking up, he saw the guard approach the cell. He held a towel.

"Here," the guard said, tossing it through the bars.

Reaching for the towel, he wiped his face, but the flour was caked on. He could taste it. It was in his ears, his nostrils, his eyelashes, everywhere. Pulling himself up, he went to the stained porcelain sink. Turning on the rusty faucet, he wet the towel. He scrubbed, struggling to get the flour paste off.

"You look like a ghost," the guard observed, peering through the bars.

Clay stared at himself in the distorted metal mirror. He did not see a face, only the reality of all that had led up to this moment. How did I let this happen? Through the caked-on flour, he saw only fragments of the man he thought he had become. Everything was in jeopardy now. He wet the towel again.

Sightings of Clay were akin to the Loch Ness Monster. It always took a few days for the story to go from the rumor mill to the mainstream press. He had to get out before then.

Outside, a rock band began playing. The jubilant noise grew louder. Sounds of song, cheers and laughter merged into one unpredictable reverberation.

Clay turned on both faucets, but the rushing water did little to drown out the noise. He scrubbed more vigorously, as if he were sanding his own skin, doing his best to focus in on any other sound than what was coming through the window.

"You're lucky to be in here," the guard shouted over the intruding music. "Two more nights of this! Crazy Italians!"

Clay did not respond. With eyes focused on the mirror, he scrubbed away.

"You're not Italian, are you?" the guard asked, realizing his own political incorrectness.

Clay shook his head no.

The guard continued to make casual conversation as he moved closer to the cell bars. He had a purpose. He was trying to see Clay's reflection in the mirror.

"You know the last night they actually dress a little girl as an angel and hang her from a rope! Three stories up! Crazy I tell you!"

Clay thought of Bella as he splashed water on his face. How am I going to get out of here, and how am I going to keep my promise to her? I should have told her the truth. There's nothing you can do.

As Clay wiped the water from his face, the guard spotted a partial view of his clean reflection.

"You're really him, aren't you?" The guard was excited, but still unsure.

Clay did not flinch. He just stared into the mirror.

"You're in a lot of trouble. Are you sure you don't want to call someone?"

Clay remained silent, running his fingers through his wet hair.

"You don't have anyone to call, do you?"

As the guard turned to leave, Clay, still staring into the

mirror, finally spoke.

"Could you get me some paper? Some paper and a pen?"

Puzzled, the guard nodded yes.

＊

The festivities from the first night of the feast died out around 1 a.m. but Clay had just started scribbling. He sat on the cement floor, the pages clasped in his hand as he wrote. It was finally quiet enough for him to listen, if not to God's voice, to his own. It was the only thing he could do. It was the only thing he knew how to do. Clay hadn't written in years, and for a moment, wondered if he could, wondered why he should bother, but what he wrote had played out in his mind a thousand times before.

He didn't know exactly what he was writing, a defense, a eulogy, a document to remind himself that he wasn't who they said he was. Everyone else would have their say tomorrow, but this was his.

Clay fell asleep on the floor, leaning up against the brick wall.

A few hours later the guard awoke him.

"You're going to the courthouse."

Clay wiped the sleep out of his eyes.

Gathering the pages he had written, he stuffed them into his back pocket before standing. He wouldn't be alone. This would be with him.

He went to the sink, splashed some water on his face and ran his fingers through his hair before turning to leave.

The holding room at the courthouse was only slightly larger than the jail cell but without windows. The arraignment was set to begin within the hour, but Clay's court-appointed lawyer had yet to show.

Pacing the room, he thought about representing himself, but knew he didn't have credibility in the court's eyes. Besides, he had been defending himself for as long as he could remember. He had been on trial his whole life, at the studio and in the court of public opinion. But this was all too sick. After all these years, after everything he did to ensure his freedom, Burt had him cornered. That twisted *SOB* had him cornered.

Clay's lawyer was on the phone when he finally arrived, shaking Clay's hand with a firm grasp, but waited until he was finished with the call before giving him his full attention.

"Don't worry. I've reviewed the case. I got this all under control," Jeffrey Spaulding said smiling. His cell rang again. "Oh sorry, this is important. Just one minute."

Clay shook his head.

Once Spaulding was off his cell, he explained his strategy. He was convinced that once it was revealed that Burt had worked on the show, the case would be dismissed. Clay was not so sure.

"This is a slam dunk!" Spaulding assured him.

Clay hated the idea that his fate was in the hands of another person, again. He thought that Jeffrey Spaulding didn't look the part of a lawyer and that he should be sent back to Central Casting. To Clay, most of what people called real life was a myth. In the end, everything was show business. And this guy lacked the believability to persuade a judge. Clay might have cast him as a *know-it-all bartender* or a *sidekick cop*, but not a lawyer. Spaulding was way too boisterous, in his crumpled suit, with an overconfidence that made Clay uneasy.

"Judges don't like me. They want to make examples of guys like me. And you don't know Burt!"

They argued back and forth, Spaulding discrediting most of what Clay said. Clay needed to hear Spaulding's "Plan B," but it was clear he didn't have one.

"Showtime," the bailiff said, opening the door.

Frustrated, Clay finally pulled out the pages he had written and circled one section before handing them to Spaulding. He knew the importance of knowing your audience, in this case, a judge.

"Use this."

Spaulding glanced at it with a patronizing stare.

To appease Clay, Spaulding refolded the pages and stuffed them into his suit pocket. "I've been doing this awhile," he assured him. "Trust me."

Clay felt the familiar panic as they walked through the door. Hearing "trust me" from a lawyer *never* ended well.

*

*

*

*

*

*

# *Chapter Ten*

The steady hum of oscillating fans filled the historic courtroom, drowning out the lawyer and prosecutor arguing before the judge during the arraignment. The air conditioning was down again and the fans were another short-term solution to an ongoing problem. It didn't help that the brick courtroom was on the third floor or that the Federal-style windows were bare, ran floor to ceiling, and that they faced the noonday sun. So on days like this, the emboldened sun poured in uninhibited by anything except the judge herself. Rotund with a constipated smile, it was obvious Judge Scott was sweltering beneath her black robe with the intense heat at her back. The golden laser beams braised her shoulder before traveling across the bench and landing in the courtroom.

This hour the sharp rays took aim at Clay. The sun blazed against his face, but he didn't flinch. Unwilling to acknowledge Burt, who sat on the other side of the courtroom, Clay felt that familiar disgust. He hadn't been in such proximity to him in years. Yet he could sense not just Burt's presence, but also his lingering feelings of anger, hatred, and resentment.

And Clay couldn't just feel him, he could hear him. Although Burt was silent, his accusing thoughts were louder than the prosecutor or the judge.

"Why is Mr. Cummings wearing a neck brace?" the judge asked.

"He injured his neck in the fall, Your Honor," the prosecutor said, straightening his bowtie.

Clay shifted uncomfortably in his seat.

Spaulding was quick to explain. "Burt Cummings charged at my client while he was unloading a truck at his place of employment."

"He hit him with a forty-pound bag of flour—"

"Self-defense—"

"With a forty-pound bag of flour?"

Chasing him from that day in the Burbank mall until now, Burt had finally caught up with him. He had Clay exactly where he wanted him, charged with assault. Clay had robbed him of his livelihood, his good name in Hollywood and his shot at *big* money. He had gotten away with the fire, but not this. Burt didn't want things to escalate to the point where another paparazzo could swoop in and profit first. He'd worked too hard to not be the one who would profit from Clay's mess. And still he couldn't help but relish that finally someone was holding Clay accountable. Finally, he would pay. Finally people would see Clay for who he really was.

"Many celebrities feel like assaulting the press, but they don't because of something called The First Amendment."

Clay looked at his lawyer. Spaulding spoke up. "Mr.

Cummings isn't just a member of the press. He previously worked on *Little Guy Mike*."

The judge glanced directly at Burt.

"He was paid by the people who effectively owned Mr. Grant, and Mr. Cummings' compensation was tied to how well he controlled him. Clay was in bondage to this man and the people he worked for."

"Owned is an overstatement," the prosecutor said. "Everything was perfectly legal. Long-term contracts for a series must be court-approved. And the law allows minors to renege on contracts signed on their behalf once they are of age."

"The legal term is disaffirmance," the judge said. She reviewed Clay's file. "Apparently, Mr. Grant's lawyer filed at age eighteen, but the court was loathe to reverse their original decision. Regardless, that all ended when the show ended. And that is not why we are here today."

"For goodness' sake, he was sold by his mother to his managers. And at eighteen they still planned on owning him. If not for the show ending, he would still be owned today. Burt Cummings made a living on my client's childhood, and is now stalking him."

"Oh, please," the prosecutor said, annoyed.

"Yes, stalking him in a further effort to exploit his celebrity for monetary gain."

Burt hoped the court didn't know he released that picture of Clay covered in flour. It was a quick buck and no one could make his face out.

"He was taking his picture. How is that a crime?"

Clay leaned over, whispering into his lawyer's ear. His

lawyer subtly motioned him to be quiet.

The prosecutor wouldn't let up. "Burt Cummings may have previously worked on the show, but he is currently a member of the press. It is still legal to take a celebrity's picture, correct?"

"Last time I checked," the judge said.

Clay knew he was in trouble.

The arraignment was underway when Reagan Mitchell stepped into the courtroom. His noble stature and steel blue eyes were softened by his endearing smile. It was a closed court, but the seventy-one-year-old inspirational pastor had a national reputation. He could motivate anyone to do just about anything. The vitality in his voice and his sturdy presence always inspired confidence. A person's shortcomings, he believed, were always problems solved with a new vision. His books were roadmaps to a better life. Lately, he questioned his own sense of direction. Reagan knew that leaving Cliff Falls now would cause friction at home, but he had a clear motive for making the cross-country journey.

Ascending the staircase, Reagan took a seat in the balcony without being noticed. Peering down at the action below, he quickly became concerned.

The judge opened Clay's case history, reviewing it aloud.

"June 'ninety-eight: creating a public disturbance, August 'ninety-nine: destruction of public property..."

"He was trying to get out of dodge, Your Honor. He was being chased by paparazzi..."

"May two thousand: mayhem, reckless driving..."

"Similar circumstances, Your Honor—"

"February two thousand one: mayhem, destruction of

private property, reckless driving. Mr. Spaulding, how many names does your client go by?"

"My client has routinely used alternate names to protect his anonymity. It's perfectly legal."

The prosecutor interrupted, "He also has a habit of skipping out on landlords."

The judge stared at Clay over her glasses. "You're *really* that little guy?" she said sarcastically.

Clay smiled at her, embarrassed.

"My client has made restitution. If you look in his file, you'll see—"

"There is always an explanation. It's always someone else's fault," the prosecutor said. "Personal responsibility," he added glancing at Clay. "That's what separates Ron Howard from Danny Bonaduce. Jodie Foster from Dana Plato. Personal responsibility."

"This court is a big fan of personal responsibility," the judge said. "If only our nation were."

Reagan knew no one could argue with that. He leaned forward, like a player on the bench dying to get in the game, ready to use his God-given talent to turn this thing around. He wanted to descend the staircase and represent Clay himself. Reagan was not a lawyer but he was capable of doing what the law could never do: persuade a crowd.

Spaulding looked lost.

The courtroom was silent except for the steady hum of the fans that resembled static on a television broadcast that had been unexpectedly interrupted.

The sun's rays were now directed at the defeated Spaulding. The heat was affecting him. Tugging at his tie, noticeable perspiration beaded upon his forehead.

"Anything else?" the judge asked.

Clay cleared his throat to get his lawyer's attention. With subtle glances and stares they argued back and forth. Finally, against his better judgment, Spaulding reluctantly reached into his suit pocket and removed the folded pages.

"If I may," he said unfolding the pages. Spaulding glanced at what Clay had circled and then read a few lines.

*"Clay is a screw-up! We're not going to argue that. If that's what you're looking for, there's plenty to find."*

Spaulding paused, maybe this was a bad idea, but the way things were looking—

*"We consume child stars twice. First, we think of them as cute dolls created for our entertainment. Then we judge them mercilessly when they grow up and stumble, all the while thinking of them as the collective property of those they once entertained.*

*"Clay is not a doll. He is not a meal ticket. He is a human being."*

Spaulding had life in his eyes, a passion that had been missing.

Reagan smiled confidently. Finally, Spaulding was humanizing Clay.

"My client is not a sympathetic figure. Look at his file,"

Spaulding conceded.

"The faxes are still coming in," the judge said, lifting the thick file.

"It's all a desperate attempt to reclaim his life,"

Spaulding said.

Clay clenched his jaw, trying not to mouth the words he had written.

"He's done everything he can do to live a quiet, normal life. It's time we left him alone."

He pointed to Burt.

"What about this man's choices? How long can someone be hunted without protection from the court?"

Spaulding was on a roll, and he knew it.

"What would they find if they dug up Mr. Cummings' past? Or mine? Or any of us here in this courtroom? I guarantee you that if they looked hard enough, they'd find what they were looking for, and plenty more."

He glanced at the page again, connecting to Clay's words as if they were his own.

"I humbly ask the court, the prosecution, Burt Cummings, 'When you look at Clay Grant, what are you looking for? Because that's exactly what you're going to find.'"

"Nice sentiment, Spaulding," the judge said. "I didn't know you had it in you."

Sensing some empathy, Clay looked at the judge hoping that she saw him as something more than a commodity.

The judge continued, "I can assure you, Mr. Grant, that this court does not view you as pop culture property."

Clay and his lawyer looked at each other, hopeful.

"Motion to dismiss granted. Further I am granting the restraining order requested against Mr. Cummings."

Clay exhaled, curious if he heard the judge correctly.

Spaulding triumphantly clasped the crumpled paper.

"No!" Burt seethed in disbelief.

"Quiet. However," the judge added, "Mr. Grant is not free to go. The federal government is not as sympathetic as this court."

The judge removed a document from the file and held it up. "Unfortunately, in your absence your estate neglected to pay the IRS on your syndication earnings. You are responsible for $478,000 in back taxes."

Clay whispered into Spaulding's ear.

"My client's estate squandered those earnings," Spaulding pleaded. "He never received any of that money."

"Regardless, the law is clear. I cannot give Mr. Grant another opportunity to run. Bail is set at $100,000." The gavel fell.

Clinging to the table for support, Clay was crushed. There was nothing he could do.

Reagan rose to his feet and exited the balcony.

"It's about time you learned this lesson," the judge stared at Clay over her glasses. "Running never makes it better."

The bailiff removed Clay from the courtroom. As Clay was led out, he could feel Burt glaring at him. Clay knew this wasn't over. Burt wasn't finished with him yet.

Reagan, now on the court floor, watched as Spaulding crumpled up the paper and lobbed it into the trash. As the judge stepped down from the bench, Reagan approached her, carrying a hardback book entitled, *The Road to Hope*.

"This is a closed court. How did you get in here?" the judge asked, looking at him suspiciously.

"Your Honor, I'm Reagan Mitchell." In hopes of establishing credibility, Reagan pointed to his own picture on the back of his book.

"You're that guy?"

"I'm that guy."

As the judge took her last step off the bench, the unforgiving light at her back filled the courtroom.

The sharp rays now took aim at Reagan, shining directly into his confident face. "May I have a moment?"

*Chapter Eleven*

Clay peered through the cell's iron-barred window as the feast continued, his eyes watching the slow moving processional. The cheering crowd marched behind the revered statue of the Madonna embracing the Little King— Mary and the boy Jesus.

The Little King sat on his mother's lap beneath an ornate canopy of gilded azure cloth on a platform the men were careful to keep steady. It was as if the Madonna, his mother, were protecting him. Like a child star, the Little King was donned in a jeweled crown and a flowing robe woven with gold thread and covered in dollar bills pinned to the cloth. Clay thought the robe looked heavy. As the statue was paraded down the street, Clay identified with the Little King, staring into his empathetic eyes, eyes that seemed to look deeply back at him. He was transported back to his youth.

*"Imagine, California. Palm trees. Sun. Everything good is*

*happening for us, and it's because of you, my little angel."*

*"But I like it here," Clay said, holding his bike in their modest Kansas studio apartment.*

*His mother tossed his suitcase on the pullout sofa bed and started packing.*

*"Can I take my bike?" Clay asked, clinging to the handlebar.*

*"Only take what you need. We'll have our things shipped later. I know it'll just be an apartment in the San Fernando Valley, but it'll be ours."*

*"School hasn't started yet!" Clay said anxiously. "I won't be able to say goodbye to my friends!"*

*"You'll make new friends. Listen, this is our new beginning. They loved the pilot. How could they not? You lit up the screen just like you light up my life. It's going to be okay. If things work out this could go on forever."*

*"But what if I can't do it?" Clay cried. "What if the audience doesn't like me?"*

*"I need you to be strong." She embraced the boy as tears streamed down his face. "Just do what they say and you'll be okay. We'll be okay."*

But we weren't.

"I didn't even get to say goodbye."

Clay's memory was abruptly interrupted when the guard entered.

"You have a visitor."

Facing the window, with hands pressed against the brick wall, Clay panicked fearing it was Burt. "I said no cameras, no visitors."

"This one posted your bail," the guard shot back, sorting

through the key ring.

Slowly, Clay turned from the window. He saw Reagan Mitchell standing beside the guard. Clay was bewildered.

"It's been a long time." Reagan smiled warmly.

The guard held up the key, waiting for his response. Clay nodded, and the guard unlocked the gate.

Reagan stepped into the cell as the guard locked the gate behind him before leaving. He cautiously engaged Clay, who was silent. "I think the last time I saw you, you were, what, sixteen?"

Reagan took a moment, searching for the boy within the man standing before him. He couldn't get over how different he looked. "If it weren't for those eyes, I don't think I could recognize you."

Clay lowered his gaze.

Reagan tried another direction, moving around the cell, avoiding direct eye contact. "That was some argument your lawyer made, 'People find what they're looking for'. A very effective line. For a moment I forgot I was in a courtroom. I felt like I was in church. A good church."

Reagan continued in his best preacher voice. "What would they find if they dug up the past of anyone of us here in the courtroom? I guarantee you that if they looked hard enough, they'd find what they were looking for, and plenty more. When you look at Clay, 'What are you looking for?' because that's exactly what you're going to find."

"Seventeen—I was seventeen."

"Yes, seventeen. We must have toured a dozen stadiums that summer. 'Just Say No'. If only life were that simple." Reagan sat on the edge of the mattress, feeling the springs of the metal bed.

"I was added to the tour after that picture of me smoking pot hit the press. The studio had a solution for every problem." Clay faced the window, peering out. "Your wife and son were on that tour, right?"

"Yes." Reagan proceeded, feeling he gained a measure of trust from Clay. "Rose never forgot you," he hesitated. "And Ted is a pastor now at our church in Cliff Falls."

"Figures. I already believe in the Good Book, if that's why you came," Clay said defensively. He never had a hard time believing in the existence of God, but they weren't exactly on speaking terms. "Try my stalker. I'm sure he can help you meet your quota."

"Stalker?"

"That guy isn't just any paparazzo. We have a history. Don't you remember? He was on the tour, and payroll. Burt. The Enforcer. He blames me for ending his career. He blames me for existing. But no one blames him."

"What really happened the night of the fire, Clay?"

"I grew up in a land of make believe, a factory really. The line between real and fake could get blurred. But on my 18th birthday some realities were too real for me to ignore, even if everyone else did." Clay caught his breath. "What happened is what always happened. Only this time, it was just too much. I had another fight with Burt. I was supposed to get the day off. Instead, the studio had me signing the new product line. Anything to line their pockets. That's when Burt told me that my mom wasn't coming. It was her choice but they pushed her out. Their goose was going to lay a golden egg even if Burt had to squeeze it out of me."

Clay ran his fingers through his hair. "Nothing was ever going to change. I just couldn't look at my face plastered on all that junk one more day. So I piled them on the backlot. Struck a match." Clay looked at Reagan. "It was just a tantrum, I didn't know it would get out of control."

"So that's why you left," Reagan empathized. "Where have you been?"

"Everywhere. Nowhere. But it didn't matter. The syndication was huge. Wherever I went 'Little Guy Mike' followed. It was three years before I figured out they covered up that I started the fire. Do you know how scared I was that whole time? I'm an idiot. I should have known protecting their cash cow was more important.

"So why are you here?" Clay asked sarcastically, "Going on tour again? Need another redemption story for the crowd?"

"Clay... I just flew 3,000 miles to remind you that you matter." Reagan rose to his feet. "Whatever trouble you are in, I am here to help."

Clay looked directly into Reagan's eyes. "What do you want?"

"In a way I feel responsible. I saw the pressure you were under, You were only a boy. I should have done something. Some adult should have done something."

"And you think you can do something now?"

"I'd like to try. It's been too long. And by the looks of things, nothing's gotten better."

Clay had only known the confident Reagan. Now as Clay looked at him he saw something different, a frailty in his steel blue eyes. Maybe he was sick, maybe he was just getting old, but Clay couldn't ignore what he saw or his sincerity. For a moment, Clay wondered if it were Reagan who needed the help.

"I can't just sit by and watch another young life wasted. You have so much potential."

Clay pointed to the jail bars. "Potential is not exactly my top priority right now. And you can save the Horatio Alger speech and leave my bootstraps alone. I have no interest in 'winning friends or influencing people'."

"You're in a lot of trouble. You are responsible for $478,000 in back taxes," Reagan said.

"I *never* saw a dime of that money! Punishment for keeping the fire a secret. How could I owe a half-million dollars when I never saw a profit? But it doesn't matter. Nothing I do matters."

"I want to help you escape all of this, if you'll let me."

Reagan put his hand on Clay's shoulder. He flinched in a knee-jerk reaction. His bum shoulder was still sensitive.

Embarrassed, Clay gripped the bars, staring blankly out of the cell. "How do you escape a life that lives in syndication? And how do you move on when people won't let you move on because of who they need you to be?"

"Do you know what you want?" Reagan realized that it was a loaded question.

"What do I want?" The truth was Clay only knew what he didn't want, but decided to indulge the man. "You know that old ship in the harbor?"

"Old Ironsides."

"I want to hijack her, take her out of the harbor. Out to sea. Set her free."

"And then what?"

"Find another place I can start over. A place I can have

peace. A place I can be really free."

"Can you envision such a place? What does it look like?"

Clay closed his eyes and painted a picture of a place he had obviously dreamed of. "It would have to have a lot of trees, kind of mountainous, like Colorado. Somewhere green. Somewhere I could exhale."

"What else?" Reagan leaned forward, coaxing him on.

"Well, it couldn't be too far from the water. I need to know if things ever got really bad, I could jump on a ship and sail away."

"Anything else?"

Clay opened his eyes. "How could I forget? There would be no television!"

Reagan laughed at the unrealistic request.

"Or at least very bad reception."

"So there is only one question left: If you knew such a place actually existed, would you have the courage to go there?"

Clay shifted uncomfortably.

"Your judge is now a friend of mine. She's agreed to release you into my custody."

"Why would the judge agree to that?"

"See sometimes 'winning friends and influencing people' comes in handy," Reagan grinned.

"There are conditions. I would pay a third of your debt to the IRS up front."

"You'd do that? That's a lot of money," Clay said with disbelief.

Reagan nodded.

"What else?" Clay said looking for the catch.

"I would provide you with a job to pay off the rest and

make a series of reports to the court."

"Doing what exactly?"

Reagan smiled. "I'll come up with something."

"I don't know."

"Believe it or not, you just described Cliff Falls right down to the lousy television reception. It's tucked in the Santa Cruz Mountains of Northern California, fifteen minutes from the ocean. It's beautiful. Trees. Hiking trails. Plenty of space to breathe. And it's green."

"I'm desperate. But a church?" He was only partially sorry for the insult. Clay pictured people waving their hands in the air like on one of those Time Life Worship CD infomercials. Good lord.

"There's a media circus waiting for you outside. Clay, you could avoid this whole thing."

"I need some time."

"I have to get back. I've been away too long as it is. A car will pick you up tonight and take you to the airport. No one will know you've been released."

"What about Burt?"

"That won't be a problem," Reagan assured him. "They have another way to get you out besides the front door. There's a tunnel that connects this jail and the building across the street. You'll be able to escape Burt and any other paparazzi."

Reagan pulled a business card out of his wallet, and handed him a few hundred dollars. "It's probably not smart to go back to your apartment."

Clay held the money in his hand. "You trust me?"

Reagan motioned to the guard who unlocked the gate.

"You're betting on the wrong horse. Google me. I'm famous

for letting people down."

"Funny thing about 'Old Ironsides' is that she's made of wood, oak from the Carolina swamp." Reagan stepped out of the cell. "Barely fifty yards apart, the Brits bombarded that ship with sixteen-pound cannon balls. And you know what? They ricocheted off. The young sailors couldn't believe their eyes when they saw that the cannon balls were simply bouncing off her hull."

The guard shut the gate.

Reagan glanced through the bars. "Who knew wood could be so strong?"

Reagan turned to leave.

"Wait. There's something I need you to do for me first. You trust me. Now I need to trust you."

Reagan looked puzzled.

∗

Reagan Mitchell stepped out of the taxi, and onto the curb. He entered the building and ascended the staircase. Apartment 2C was down the hall. He retrieved the key from the light box and unlocked the door.

Stepping inside, the saltbox was more of a closet than an apartment. The smell of seawater poured in through the porthole window. Moving forward, Reagan ignored the stuffed duffel bag on the floor, wondering if Clay always kept it packed in the event he had to leave town quickly.

Crossing to the bed, Reagan lifted the mattress and discovered a burnt journal with a rope tied around it. He was bewildered.

Against his better judgment, he untied the rope and a page fell out. Before retrieving the page, he read the inscription on the inside cover.

*"To Clay: The right words at the right time can change everything. I believe. Rose Mitchell."*

Overwhelmed, Reagan crouched down and retrieved the page from the floor. As he read it, he became engrossed.

*"It happened again."*

Reagan caught his breath. It was a description of abuse.

*"All I ever want to be is a thousand miles away from anyone who can hurt me. Dear God. Just give me one chance and I swear I will never look back. This time no one will find me."*

He didn't feel right reading anymore. He shut the journal and looked out the window at the waiting taxi. In the distance he saw Old Ironsides moored in the harbor.

\*

Clay was released in the early morning hours. Just as Reagan promised, he was escorted downstairs through a series of narrow corridors that led from the jail to the building across the street. Two rusty metal sheet doors covering a deep hole in the sidewalk opened. Clay emerged into the alley that had police barricades on either side.

The North End was still except for the sweeper truck that drove past him, clearing the road of trash from the feast the night before. For the moment he was safe. He paused on the corner, checking his pocket for the cash Reagan gave him. What is this guy up to? What makes him think I won't take the money and run? This time nobody will find me.

Further down the street, Clay noticed the rope and pulley in the town square. He couldn't help but think of Bella, wondering if she would be all right. He had made a promise to her. Someone had to reassure the little girl that she could do it, that those ropes would hold her.

Clay watched as the first news van set to cover the Angel Flight pulled into the North End. Pulling his navy knit hat lower, he moved on.

# Chapter Twelve

Documents flapped beneath paperweights as the 1960's metal fan blasted the counter in the clerk's office before rotating and refreshing the line of people seated in the waiting area. The ancient fan with woven cord was a fire hazard, justified as another short-term solution.

In the back office, a distracted jail clerk held a hundred-dollar bill in his hand as Burt struggled in vain to find information of Clay's release.

"That's all I know," the clerk insisted, shuffling through his files. "You're really fixated on this guy. Are you some kind of stalker?"

"Who posted his bail?" Burt pressed, waving two more Ben Franklins. He had cash on hand from a few small-time paparazzi jobs and didn't mind doling it out in hopes of a bigger return. Local news vans were already filling the streets of the North End. The national press couldn't be far behind.

"It was a 'special arrangement of the court'. Only the

judge knows."

"You're telling me no one, except for the judge, knows where he is?"

"Maybe you should ask the angel?"

"The angel?"

"The kid from the bakery. Don't you watch the local news? That was his only friend."

The clerk reached into a file, and then held up Clay's mug shot, waving it tauntingly at Burt. "He won't be in hiding for long. Not after this is released. Of course, that would make any photo you take worthless," the clerk smirked, fanning himself with the mug shot.

Burt knew the guy was bluffing. "This district doesn't release mug shots to the public. I already checked."

"Not officially. But these shots do have a way of getting leaked to the press," the clerk taunted again.

"I'll give you a grand to lose that photo."

## Chapter Thirteen

The Fisherman's Feast and Angel Flight banner was illuminated with strings of glowing lights. Below, a brass band played as the massive crowd filled the narrow streets and sidewalks in anticipation of the grand finale. Since 1911, the soaring pronouncement was the same: the young angel's petition to the Madonna for the fishermen's safe return home from sea.

The crowd shouted, "Viva! Madonna!"

Bella peered out the third story window. Practicing her Italian prayer, her angelic voice trembled as she repeated each line. Word had gotten out about Clay's release. She just knew he was there somewhere, but she couldn't spot him among the faces in the crowd.

Angelo zipped Bella's blue angel dress.

"He promised he'd be here."

"It's not possible," Angelo said. "He's in a lot of trouble."

"He'll be here. I know it. He would have said goodbye."

"All these people came to see you," Bella's father said, placing the gold crown on her curly locks. He pressed it down, securing it with bobby pins.

"It's too tight!" Bella said, squinting.

Her father was unmoved. "Smile, Bella. Smile!"

Bella glanced out the window, forcing a nervous smile.

"In just a few moments one lucky girl will make the traditional flight on this, the last night of the Fisherman's Feast," the reporter said into the camera. "I am now standing with Angelo De Spirito who is not only the father of this year's angel, but the manager of this landmark bakery. Did you have any idea 'Little Guy Mike' was working in your bakery?"

"I only watch *M*A*S*H* and *Who's the Boss*? If Tony Danza worked in my bakery, I'd know it."

"Do you have any indication where he went?" the reporter pressed. "Has he tried to make contact with you or your daughter?"

Angelo shrugged his shoulders, wanting attention kept on his daughter, not Clay.

Burt was milling about in the crowd. His camera was tucked on the inside of his jacket. He wasn't about to let a restraining order stop him. He got another tip on how close Clay was to the little girl playing the angel and wouldn't put it past him to show up.

Bella sat on the windowsill with her back to the crowd, gripping her fragrant bouquet. Men on the fire escape attached the wooden pulley to the harness hidden beneath her flowing blue-and-white gown. They tied ropes to her legs to help maintain her body position once in the air.

The crowd shouted again, "Viva! Madonna!"

This was the moment. Bella squeezed her eyes shut as she was yanked out the window, her outstretched arms shaking as she was hoisted above the masses. Despite the shouts and cheers of the crowd, she could still hear her father's voice.

"They love you, Bella! Smile for the people! Smile!"

She forced a smile, refusing to open her eyes. As she hovered above the crowd, the ropes tied to her legs steadied her into position. She knew it was time.

Opening her eyes, Bella was overwhelmed by the crowd of blurry faces surrounding her. They were everywhere. In the streets. Peering out their apartment windows. On the rooftops. Her throat tightened as her body trembled with fear. Bella searched the faces on the rooftops but couldn't find Clay anywhere. Where is he?

Burt, on the ground, saw her looking. He scanned the rooftops.

They lowered Bella to the Madonna and child to begin the prayer. The canopied statue was completely covered in dollar bills pinned to the flowing ribbons.

"The prayer, Bella! The prayer!" Angelo shouted.

She heard her father yelling, but it didn't matter. Although she had practiced the prayer a thousand times before, she could not remember it. Perhaps it was the sight of the crowd, or possibly that she had been praying another prayer, a desperate plea for help and courage, as she was yanked out the window. It was a prayer without words but one that was stronger than any she had prayed before. It was so real that now a prayer with words was as foreign to her as flying above the crowd. She searched the eyes of the Madonna and child statue pleading for help but she could not remember the proclamation.

"It seems as if our angel has forgotten her prayer," the reporter said into the camera. The scores of people waited. You could hear a pin drop.

"Say something, Bella! Say something. Anything!" Angelo cried with embarrassment.

Finally, Bella spoke, recalling Clay's words. "I didn't choose this!" she shouted, dangling above the multitude.

The crowd had a collective look of confusion.

"I didn't!" Bella said. She prayed for courage. "But I'm up here. So..."

The crowd hung on her every word, waiting for her to finish the sentiment.

"I might as well fly!"

Bella nodded to the men working the ropes. Within moments she began to move, flying back and forth, soaring over the crowd. "I might as well fly!"

The spectators cheered as she picked up speed, soaring over the narrow streets, the wind blowing against her face. "I might as well fly!"

People on the rooftops threw shreds of white paper onto the crowd, the confetti filling the sky and covering the streets.

"Out of the mouths of babes," the reporter said into the camera. "Quite a turn of events in the North End. A new prayer at the Angel Flight and a confirmation that 'Little Guy Mike' was indeed working at Mike's Pastry. Unbelievable. I guess the only question left is, 'Where is "Little Guy Mike"'?"

Across the way in an empty building, a man in sunglasses and a navy knit hat watched from the rooftop. As the crowd dispersed, Burt looked up and spotted him. Yes!

Pushing his way through the crowd, he darted into the building. Burt raced up the steps, positioning his camera. He had blown the element of surprise at the bakery. He wouldn't make the same mistake twice. As Burt burst through the door, the man's back was just in front of him. The perfect picture was just a tap on the shoulder away.

Readying his camera with one hand, he reached out with the other....

*Chapter Fourteen*

Startled, Clay felt a hand on his shoulder as the flight attendant awakened him.

"Sir, your seat. You need to bring it back up."

Squinting at her below the rim of his knit hat, he nodded. Clay raised his seat, glancing around the cabin. It killed him that he broke his promise to Bella but what could he do. They each had their own flight to make. *How am I going to fix this with her? I'll probably never see her again.*

Clay had to leave while he could. The media was everywhere. Luckily, the car that picked him up got him out in time. At the airport, the ticket was waiting for him, along with his duffel bag. But when Clay unzipped it, his journal wasn't among the items. He prayed that Reagan had gotten to it first and not Burt. If Reagan did have it, Clay knew he held on to it for safekeeping, or insurance that he would arrive. Hopefully, Clay hadn't made a mistake trusting him.

The landing gear rumbled beneath his feet.

"This is the Captain. We have begun our descent into SFO. The temperature is a cool 57 degrees. We should be on the ground in twenty minutes."

Through the fogged window, the illuminated skyline emerged behind pockets of thick clouds. He focused on the city landscape below. He was searching for the place Reagan described. I don't see any mountains. Strike one?

The taxi exited the airport and banked south onto Highway 101, where it merged into a wall of glowing brake lights.

"Traffic always this bad?"

"You should have seen it during the technology boom," the cabbie said, glancing in the rear-view mirror. "Back then, even I worked at a startup."

Clay cracked the window open. The smell of exhaust filled his nostrils. Plenty of room to breathe? Strike two. Cliff Falls is probably an office complex on top of Nob Hill.

"Hold on." The cabbie maneuvered into the breakdown lane.

Clay grabbed the door railing.

The taxi accelerated down the expressway, heading west at sunset.

The cabbie pointed out the window. "That's where we're going. Highway 280. They call this the most beautiful highway in the world."

Clay spotted a mountain range in the distance, glowing in a backdrop of deep purple and orange hues. A blanket of sturdy trees lined the rugged ridges. He rolled down the window the rest of the way and felt the vigorous breeze against his face.

Accelerating past fields of horses and cattle before climbing upward, the taxi wound the narrow mountain road, ascending with the native redwoods and mighty oaks. Maybe Reagan was telling the truth?

Clay leaned forward. A carved wooden marker read:

## WELCOME TO CLIFF FALLS
## ESTABLISHED 1884

The taxi traveled down the main street, which was pocketed with rustic, ranch-style buildings peeking through the foliage.

Walnut Grove meets Mayberry? This place was so appealing that it looked like it was built on the studio backlot. Clay half wondered if real businesses were behind those charming storefronts or if the streets ended abruptly once they curved out of sight.

"Where in Cliff Falls?" the cabbie asked.

"A church...High Hope Community." Clay pulled out a business card but the cabbie knew where it was.

"I don't care what they say," the cabbie spoke into the rear-view mirror. "I think that Reagan is a good guy."

Clay returned a puzzled look. Strike three?

They drove along Ridge Road as night fell. Just ahead, he saw the light of the church sign:

## HIGH HOPE COMMUNITY CHURCH
## A FAMILY FOR YOU!

For a moment Clay allowed himself to imagine having a real family but he knew better than to put stock in a tagline. He had made that mistake before.

The cabbie pulled into a crowded parking lot and stopped.

All the cars surprised Clay. "What's going on here tonight?"

"Something big, I think," the cabbie said. "Should I let you out here?"

He paid the cabbie and then stepped out of the taxi onto the gravel pavement. Despite the cars, no one was in sight.

"It's up there." The cabbie pointed to an illuminated cross at the top of the hill.

"Wait here," Clay said, putting on his backpack and reaching for his duffel bag. If things went south, he wanted a clean escape. He was miles from civilization, on top of a mountain range and knew he wouldn't be able to make his way back now that it was dark.

"I've got to get back to the city—"

"Just a few minutes," Clay insisted, shutting the door.

Walking upward along the curving pathway, he made his way toward the front of the church. The wind rustled through the trees.

Don't overreact just because there are a million cars here. It's probably BINGO night. He took a few steps and stopped.

"Wait, only Catholics play BINGO."

Moving up the hill, he spotted the white steeple, a vague reminder of the Old North Church, holding up the cross above the trees. It was the only light, save the craftsman-style lanterns that lined the path. Gripping his duffel bag, Clay did his best to ignore the uneasy sense of foreboding as deadened leaves crunched beneath his feet.

Are we out of strikes yet?

He told himself that it wasn't too late to turn back. But the truth was he could never go back. That was one lesson he learned early on. He had been so many places over these fifteen years, but back was never one of them.

As Clay crested the hill, bright lights blinded him, stopping him in his tracks.

He strained his blurry eyes and spotted the media in the glow of the white clapboard church. Crews filled the lawn. Cameramen with equipment resting on their shoulders awaited the cue while reporters with microphones in hand prepared for the live remote.

"News vans! He didn't?"

He looked down the hill. The taxi was gone. Desperate, Clay took cover behind a protective oak tree. His heart raced. He struggled to catch his breath as he pressed against the coarse bark.

"You son of a bitch. You set me up!"

# Chapter Fifteen

Pressing his face against the bark, Clay peeked around the oak at the hungry media. *This is what I get for trusting Reagan. A step of faith right into a ditch!*

"That's not a very good hiding place," a boy said, wheezing.

Turning abruptly, Clay's cheek scraped as it pulled away from the bark. He looked down. The boy, maybe nine years old, was standing beside him, tugging at his tie.

Still wheezing, the boy stared at Clay through a blond mop top that had been styled with a wet comb. He was dressed like a miniature accountant in a crisp white shirt and navy striped tie. Gasping for air, he emptied his khakis' left pocket, tossing the contents onto the ground: a pack of bubble gum, a hand-held video game, and a few baseball cards.

"Excuse me?" Clay said, as he ducked back behind the tree.

Reaching into the other pocket, the boy found it! Giving his asthma inhaler a good shake, he gave himself a solid burst of air. "I said," the boy spoke slowly, emphasizing his point, "that's-not-a-very-good-hiding-place."

"Who said I'm hiding?" Clay shot back, careful to keep his voice down so as not to draw attention.

"The church balcony is your best bet." The boy glanced over his shoulder, pointing at the church, trying to untie his tie. "But don't stay there too long 'cause after a while they come looking for you there, too!"

Clay turned his head toward the church. In front of him was a media circus ready to exploit him. Behind him was this kid who had seen right through him. The rustling of dead leaves at his back interrupted Clay's despair. He turned.

The boy now resembled a determined, but misdirected Houdini. Spinning in the dirt, he frantically tugged at the diminished, but stronger knot in his tie. The harder he pulled, the tighter the knot became.

"Easy!" Clay said. He dropped his duffel bag to the ground. "Is it okay if I help you?" He was careful to ask first, something adults rarely did when he was a kid.

The boy nodded repeatedly, his grateful blue eyes dilated.

"Relax," Clay said as he worked the knot. "The secret is to relax."

The boy rolled his eyes, incapable of relaxing while constrained in this formal garb.

"Point taken." Clay smiled. "Ever heard of a clip-on?" The tips of his fingers separated the twisted tie. "You know if you lose this they can't make you wear it. I just think a kid should know his options."

The tie came undone. The boy exhaled, letting out a loud gasp. "I can breathe! I can breathe!" He stood up dizzily, untucking his shirt, inhaling the night air.

"Tyler!" a woman's voice hollered in the distance.

The boy's eyes widened.

"Tyler!" the voice screamed louder.

Clay watched as Tyler gasped for air.

"Here!" the boy whispered, thrusting his tie at Clay. Reaching down, he grabbed his baseball cards, bubble gum, and video game, and crammed them back into his pockets. Then, running in the opposite direction from the voice, he called back to Clay, "You never saw me!"

Sliding back behind the tree, Clay watched the boy veer down a trail and disappear into the darkness. He was envious, recalling a time when he could disappear that fast. Clay looked at the navy striped tie in his hand. Searching for a place to hide it, he finally stuffed it in his back pocket. As he inched his body around the perimeter of the tree, the woman passed on the other side on her way down the hill.

The kid was right; this tree wasn't going to conceal him all night. He looked back at the reporters, wondering if Burt was among them.

Clay banged his head against the mighty oak, his punishment for being so gullible. The impression of bark on his forehead began to sting.

He was confident that Reagan had coordinated this reception from Boston. Hell, he probably took out ads in the local newspaper. *High Hope Reforms Wayward Child Star.* That'll drive attendance. And it almost worked, too. He felt the sudden weight of his backpack as he adjusted the straps.

Sitting in that jail, he hadn't seen it. Reagan pulled off the impossible: insincere sincerity. And they call me the actor!

He knew he needed to make a run for it. *How am I going to*

find my way down the mountain in the dark?

Just as he was about to dart down the hill, he heard the haunting music of bagpipes coming from the church.

Bagpipes? A brass band, trumpets, maybe something assembled for a supermarket opening... but bagpipes?

His eyes welled up with a mixture of anger and fear as the music seeped in. It was a fitting score to the events of the last week. He had actually believed that someone cared about him. "Why are all my green pastures Astroturf?"

The sudden glow of headlights crossed his path. A black hearse moved slowly across the lawn. News cameras were positioned on either side, filming as it progressed to the church.

Confused, Clay felt guilty that he had assumed Reagan betrayed him and that the media had turned out to see him. Okay, so maybe the world doesn't revolve around me? But who else could garner such a turnout? Wait a minute. Reagan? There was something different about Reagan. But this?

The hearse parked at the far side of the church. He watched as the pallbearers unloaded the casket. Once it was inside, the glaring lights from all the media went out.

The church was now illuminated by its own light, a few discreet fixtures that cast the structure in a warming glow. It looked modest now but more inviting, standing out from the darkness that surrounded it.

The media had gotten their money shot and were packing up for the night. It was just a matter of time before they headed his way. He thought about jetting down the hill while he could, but he needed to know if Reagan was in that casket.

Avoiding the news vans by ducking into the nearby shrubbery, he navigated on his hands and knees. Tyler wasn't the only one who had skills maneuvering unnoticed. Clay was the original phantom kid. Which could be hard when you were around someone who could smell fear. Burt would be screaming for Clay as the whole set waited, unaware that he was crawling along the rafters above or curled up in a hanging black curtain behind the set. Clay took pride in knowing that he could be right next to the guy and he wouldn't even know it. There would always be a steep price to pay for disappearing but Clay felt that those few moments of being invisible were well worth it. Clay now emerged from a row of bushes and discreetly slipped into the church through a side door.

He stepped into the lobby and was relieved to find it empty. Everyone was inside the sanctuary.

The towering sanctuary doors were hand-carved from oak. Together they formed a twisted, wind-bent tree with narrow branches filled with leaves blowing in the wind. He thought about the irony of killing a tree to carve a picture of one.

Grasping the iron handle, Clay cracked the door open.

The sea of blackness filled the sanctuary. Standing rows of dark suits and dresses spilled into the aisles. Side by side they stood, blocking his view.

As the crowd seated, Clay could see white roses draped over the simple cedar casket. It was perched on the altar, surrounded by rose bushes in stone urns.

Holding the door steady, he thought about stepping inside, but was unwilling to cross that threshold.

He let go of the rustic iron handle, and stepped back,

allowing the sturdy door to close silently. Once more he stared at the elaborate tree carving. He wanted to leave right then but he couldn't. He needed to know who was in that coffin.

# Chapter Sixteen

Stepping away from the door, Clay noticed the velvet rope with a sign that read: "Balcony Closed".

Recalling Tyler's sage advice that the balcony was a better hiding place, he stepped over the velvet rope.

Ascending the partially carpeted wooden staircase, Clay emerged into the balcony loft. It was empty except for a small tech crew running the light and soundboard that glowed in the dark. Luckily, the college-age technicians were too distracted to bother with him.

Moving forward, he stepped over twisted cables and extension cords that crossed his path. The cold night breeze from the open stained glass window brushed against his face, the tattered curtains gently blowing.

The two curtains hung over the stained glass to keep out the light, and looked as if they had once been a single curtain torn down the middle.

Above, an ominous crack in the plaster brazed the

ceiling and skirted the central beam. Earthquake damage? Several inches wide, it ran across the balcony, supporting the roof. The crack was only visible from the balcony or by those standing in the pulpit, but went unseen by the scores of people who faced the altar below. From the audience's perspective everything looked perfect. Clay wondered if the people below were in danger. Could another shake finish the job?

Watching from the balcony, Clay waited anxiously. He had promised himself that he wouldn't get his hopes up, but he had. Somewhere between the jail cell and the plane ride, he started to believe what Reagan described was real. Now he feared all that hope was sealed in that cedar casket. Leaning over the railing, he stared at the service below, searching for Reagan, terrified by what he might discover.

Finally, the door on the far side of the altar opened. The crowd rose to its feet. Clay jerked forward to see who would enter.

*

In the green room, Ted Mitchell stared into the oval mirror, struggling with his tie. His eyes were once more distracted by his father's ever-present reflection in the glass.

Reagan stood several feet away holding Ted's suit jacket.

"The Great Reagan Mitchell. Your timing is so convenient," Ted said, frustrated as he undid the uneven tie. They were the first words he had spoken to his father since his return. "I should have known."

"Son..."

"Like you'd miss an entrance." Ted couldn't get his tie straight.

"Listen—"

"Don't talk to me! I don't want to hear it."

Ted had practiced the eulogy, hastily piecing it together from memorable tributes he had heard over the years. Growing up in a church, he attended a lot of funerals. It was the sort of tribute he had waited his whole life to give, but it would not be read. It would remain folded in his suit pocket. His father would now be doing the honors. Being replaced last minute always upset Ted but this was unforgivable.

Reagan looked at his watch, put down Ted's jacket and walked over behind him. Without asking, he calmly reached around and began to re-tie Ted's tie. Reagan's face was clearly reflected in the mirror. "The secret is line up both sides. Over, then under."

Normally, when Ted wore a tie it was under a robe so he didn't have to worry about the length being even.

"She always used to do this for me. I can't believe she's gone."

"Everything changes after tonight," Reagan said softly, staring into the mirror.

"Everything has already changed," Ted said.

Ted reached into his pocket, removing the eulogy he had written, clenching it. "I would have been fine without you. You do know that?" Ted wanted his father to agree.

"We all need a little help," Reagan said, tightening the tie just below Ted's neck. Their grieving eyes glanced up, staring into the oval mirror, a telling portrait of father and son.

"The church is packed. There must be five news vans here,"

Reagan said. He turned to Ted, "Are you ready?"

Ted took a deep breath.

*

Reagan emerged from the door, his stoic face filling the television monitors. The camera stayed on him as he walked the length of the altar, the lens ignoring Ted, who followed a few paces behind.

"Thank God, it isn't him!" Clay sunk into his seat, relieved to see Reagan. I can't take much more of this. The advantage of living a life on the run is that you can stay one step ahead of sadness.

It wasn't until Clay exhaled that he realized how upset he had become. He felt like an idiot getting so worked up but who could blame him? As he slid deeper into the crushed velvet seat, his eyes glanced at the nearest monitor. All Reagan had done was walk across the altar and he had already captivated the crowd. This guy is indestructible.

Ted took the pulpit and read the 23rd Psalm.

*"The Lord is my shepherd, I shall not be in want. He makes me lie down in green pastures; he leads me beside quiet waters. He restores my soul."*

Looking into the monitor, Clay stared at Ted's close-up. It had been years, but he looked exactly the same, only taller and more polished. Just not authentic. You could stare into his eyes all day and still not know what was behind them.

"Bad lighting," Clay mumbled under his breath. Although the pulpit lights were probably positioned for Reagan, Clay thought Ted would appear unnatural in any set-up. Either Ted didn't have that inner quality that made him radiate, or he was holding his cards too close to his chest. All that did come across was that he was trying too hard. His posture, sweeping hand gestures and tilt in his head looked like he was doing a poor imitation of his father. Good grief! If you stuck a patch over his eye and put a parrot on his shoulder, you could stick him in the *Pirates of the Caribbean* ride at Disneyland. *Almost lifelike.*

Ted was halfway through the 23rd Psalm when Clay realized he hadn't heard a word Ted said. "Isn't this the one about 'green pastures and quiet waters'?" Clay felt sorry for the grieving family. Certainly, Ted wasn't doing the job.

Clay evaluated the production value of the event, forgetting that this was real, that someone had actually died. It was like when Clay would watch a monitor on set. Although he would be in full makeup and costume, he would become so engrossed that, for a moment, he would forget that it was happening live, just a few feet away, and think he was in his living room. Clay wouldn't realize he was actually on set until someone messed up or until he'd hear the director yell, "cut". Then he would snap out of it.

"Is the box open?"

Clay turned abruptly. The boy's voice had startled him.

Tyler stood in the aisle, his dress shirt wrinkled, his hair ruffled, his pants dirt-stained. He now looked like a boy his age should except for the hesitation in his eyes. He asked again. "Is the box open?"

Recognizing the boy's fear, Clay looked over the balcony and then at the boy. "It's closed. I promise."

"Everyone is here because of my grandmother."

"I'm sorry." Clay didn't know what else to say. And somehow sorry didn't seem to be enough. It wasn't that Clay wasn't sorry; it was just that there are different kinds of sorry. Clay was sorry in the way a person is when they hear about trapped miners on the evening news. Sorry from the comfort and safety of your living room as opposed to the sorry you feel standing outside the mine. Clay tried to stay clear of the mine.

The boy bravely looked out over the balcony, exhaling at what he didn't see. He sank into his seat and plopped his arm onto Clay's armrest.

"Shouldn't you be with your mother?"

"She's in New Jersey. Graduate school," the boy said remorsefully. "She didn't come." Cocking his head, he pointed over the balcony, to the empty chair on the altar. "I'm supposed to be down there."

Glancing in that direction, Clay assumed that "down there" meant in the first few rows of the church.

Tyler kicked off his penny loafers and stretched out his toes. He had been running all night because he didn't want to be up front. Not on this night, not when he was so sad. He knew that he'd be in trouble the next day, but he didn't care. He was always in trouble.

Reagan took the pulpit. Everyone in the crowd seemed to sit up straighter, including Clay and Tyler.

Although he was solemn, Reagan's face radiated in the monitors. He didn't need good lighting. He came with his own. His mere presence inspired confidence.

"Forty years ago we came to Cliff Falls with little more than a dream. Today each of you is part not only of that dream, but of our family."

"That's my grandfather," Tyler said proudly, pointing at Reagan.

Clay pulled his eyes away from the screen. "That's your grandfather?"

"Yup."

"Your grandmother was Rose Mitchell?" Clay felt a lead ball in his stomach, realizing that this was her funeral. That was a real mother. "I knew her. I'm so sorry."

The boy's eyes welled up with tears. "I'm not bad, am I? That I didn't want to be down there in front of all those people?"

"No. Your grandmother would understand."

"Now we are sad..." Reagan seemed lost for a moment, staring at the flower-draped coffin, "...but our hope remains high." Reagan lifted his head in a sweeping movement, raising his chin above the crowd, proudly echoing the sentiment. "Our hope remains high!"

Clay stared at Reagan's glossy steel eyes in the monitor, now recognizing that same frailty he had seen in that jail cell in Boston.

"Fade to black," the tech crew whispered behind him.

As the house lights faded, bagpipes played while flickering home movies appeared on screen.

Clay and Tyler sat side by side, like two kids in the movie balcony, captivated by the tribute footage celebrating the life of Rose and the history of High Hope. The black-and-white childhood images, dancing with specs, blossomed into the muted colors of faded home movies: groundbreaking, construction, the birth of Ted. They merged into the harshly lit video clips of the eighties and nineties, prayer meetings, book signings, family gatherings, the birth of Tyler. The anthem built, the sweeping music intensifying, but refusing to crest.

Instead of watching the television monitors, Clay focused on the only patch of darkness out of reach from the glare of the televisions. Through the dim light of the church, Clay watched a stoic Reagan and Ted mourn.

Clay resisted what was welling up inside of him, trying not to get overwhelmed or to feel too deeply. But it was no use. Reality set in. He felt himself crossing the threshold, connecting with the life, pain and grief of this church. He wasn't simply watching it; he was entering it, somehow standing outside the mine, waiting for word that they would be all right.

"That's my mom!" Tyler pointed at the Jumbotron in the distance.

Clay's eyes rose to the massive screen above Reagan and Ted. The digital image was so clear that it was lifelike. The vivid footage was of a family picnic. Rose was laughing in the brightness of the afternoon sun. Tyler and his mother fought over a slice of watermelon. Tugging back and forth, his mother resorted to tickling the boy. The boy was laughing, but refusing to let go.

"That's my mom," Tyler quietly repeated, mesmerized by his mother's image in the distance.

Pulling his eyes away from the screen, Clay watched the boy beside him. He recognized something familiar, too familiar in his eyes.

*His tears were obscured by the steady beads of rain traveling down the bus station window, his mother's image fading in the distance. She moved towards the bus, ticket in hand, her words repeating in his head.*

*"It's not forever. I'm in the way."*

*A moment ago, she was beside him. Now she was leaving. As she turned to walk away, he had tried to follow, but had felt a callous hand on his shoulder holding him back. "No!" the boy screamed, his objection fogging up the glass. "No!"*

*Standing with Burt was Clay's on-set tutor who had just become his part-time caretaker; and who, along with Burt, was more interested in taking than caring.*

*But there was nothing he could do. Through that blurry, rain-soaked window, Clay watched his mother get on the bus, her last words haunting him for years to come.*

*"They are going to take good care of you. I promise."*

*Suddenly, the doors shut and the bus drove away.*

"That was my mom," Tyler said softly, the image fading from the screen.

"I know."

This moment became real, too real, for Clay, no longer an observer, overwhelmed by Tyler's longing for his mother. He wasn't standing outside the mine; he was in it, trapped, gasping for air. He never wanted to enter that place again. His heart was pounding. His survival instincts told him to leave. Reaching for his duffel bag and backpack, he rose to his feet.

Since the night of the fire, he had arranged his whole life to never feel this kind of pain again, and he was not going to start now. He didn't sign up for this.

"You're leaving?" Tyler didn't have to wait for the answer.

He knew.

"I've stayed too long already."

Reluctantly, Clay reached into his back pocket, retrieving Tyler's necktie. He placed it onto the armrest beside the boy.

"I'm sorry."

Tyler looked at the tie. "I know."

Struggling to maintain his composure, Clay waved goodbye to Tyler and left. He descended the staircase and stepped into the lobby.

Determined not to return, Clay slipped out of the church. As music poured out of the sanctuary, Clay Grant walked into the night.

# Chapter Seventeen

"She was the life of this church."

Ted embraced the next mourner, his eyes aware of the ever-growing crowd that waited in line to offer condolences. It was endless. He wanted to be anywhere but here. He wondered who was being comforted.

With each hug, he felt the folded eulogy on the inside of his suit pocket press up against his chest. He hadn't read it and somehow it was repeatedly being stuffed back into his heart. It was a steady and familiar reminder from the crowd. One that undermined every "I'm sorry" that he heard. From now on, he would keep everything that close.

Ted held each embrace as long as he could; it minimized the conversation and allowed the backed-up line to move along. The sentiments and questions were becoming predictable.

"Where's Quinn?"

"She missed her flight," Ted assured the inquirer, nodding

his head with disappointment. He could tell that other people in line were listening. "She had gone back for the first day of classes."

"Quinn is lucky to have such a supportive husband."

Ted held the smile as long as he could. It was another awkward moment extended by the backed-up line. *That* he blamed on his father.

Reagan stood a few feet away, unaware that he was the cause of the slow-moving line and Ted's awkward moments. He was working the crowd as only Reagan could, and, as usual, they loved it. He was careful not to just hug the mourners, but also to touch each one on the shoulder, look into their eyes, and receive what they had to say. He gave each mourner the sort of personal attention that allowed them to walk away feeling filled up. He had a reputation as "Comforter in Chief".

But Ted knew his father. He could tell if Reagan was distracted even when others thought they had the pastor's full attention. Reagan had a way of making people feel like he was in the middle of the storm with them, even though he was never anywhere near it. As the mourners finally moved down the line, Ted noticed a familiar gleam in his father's eyes. Ted was puzzled. Reagan was looking for someone in the crowd. Who is he looking for?

Ted was standing now, but the night everything happened, he had been running.

*Tyler tried to keep up as Ted urgently raced down the hospital corridor, his father's voicemail trailing in his head. "It's time."*

*Pressing the elevator button again, Ted didn't want to miss the last moments. As they approached the nurse's station, Tyler* spotted a physician, but Ted already knew. The thick door was cracked open, the foot of the bed peeking out from the hanging curtain. It was too late. After all the days and hours Ted had spent at that hospital, in the end he was too late.

Ted stared at the door, hesitating before he moved forward. He could hear Tyler behind him, crying, being comforted by the nurse.

Ted cautiously opened the door and crossed the threshold, the stale hospital smell overwhelming him. He drew back the curtain. Her body was covered with a white sheet. As he approached the bed, his disposition was that of a scared child trying to be brave. Reaching out, he tugged at the linen covering her face. What he saw was his own face reflected back at him, the narrow nose and rounded cheekbones. Ted stared at his mother's lifeless body: the woman who gave him life, suddenly was gone.

Full of confusion, Ted looked up and turned to the nurse who was entering the room. He had one question. "Where's my father?"

# *Chapter Eighteen*

The bell jingled as Clay opened the glass door and stepped into the Acorn Diner. The chill of the night lingered on his face. His troubled eyes tried to hold back everything he was feeling inside. He had seen the diner's light from the top of the hill as he made his way down Ridge Road on foot. Only a few cars had passed him, so he was certain that he was ahead of the crowd. Be quick, Clay. Be quick.

Most establishments in Cliff Falls were closed for the night. The modest downtown was dark, except for the warming glow emanating from the Acorn Diner. It was always open late. Located at the prominent intersection of Cliff Falls Drive and Ridge Road, the yellow ranch-style building was hard to miss.

A counter ran the length of the establishment, flanked by plate-glass windows that framed the activity off each street: the one that ran through the city and the other that led up to the church. Folks eating the same food inside the same diner could have entirely different experiences; depending upon which window they were looking out. Cliff Falls Drive was usually busy, bustling with people and cars, while Ridge Road was slower and rustic, lined with towering oaks. You could enter the diner from either side; however, most people exited the door they entered.

At this hour, the streets looked the same. There was only darkness outside as mourners began trickling in. The Acorn had gotten word about the rescheduled funeral service and its unusual time, so they were expecting a crowd once the service let out. Clay clasped his duffel bag as the door slowly shut. All I need now is a phonebook and a place to wait until the cab arrives.

There was an empty seat at the counter, but Clay wasn't in the mood for small talk. He spotted a booth on the opposite side of the diner beneath the window that faced Cliff Falls Drive. He'd wait for his cab there. He knew people would be coming in the Ridge Road side of the diner and wanted to be as far away from it as possible. Reaching for a menu, he made his way across the room.

An art-deco mural adorned the wall above the counter. It depicted the town's early days: the intersection of Cliff Falls Drive and Ridge Road in the 1930's. Even then the streets were different. Clay assumed the building had been a feed store. Technically, it still was, just a different kind of feed and flock.

The mural's red and golden tones resembled the bountiful labels you'd find on the side of fruit crates from that era, but with almost a political message of brotherhood. It featured the rustic faces of city workers and ranch hands crossing paths in front of the feed store, the painted sunrays shining down on both. Clay had seen similar style murals on the East Coast, but nothing with this landscape. He admired it, but wondered if the diversity was representative of the time or imposed by the idealism of the artist.

Tossing his bag onto one side of the booth, he loosened the straps on his backpack. The shifting of its weight caused his tired eyes to look upward. It was a glimpse of Heaven. Maybe the only Heaven he would ever know. The ceiling was littered with a multitude of colorful toothpicks apparently placed there with the assistance of a straw and some hot air. Their gleaming cellophane glare was a welcome comfort to the ever-increasing sea of blackness as mourners began pouring in. Apparently, Clay wasn't as far ahead of the crowd as he thought.

Clay quickly settled into the booth, sliding all the way in until he was up against the window. He propped up his menu on one side of him, and reached for the Venetian blind, lowering it. Gazing out the window as the blinds inched down, Clay's breath on the glass was proof that his heart was still racing. He had come all this way. He felt terrible skipping out on Reagan, but he couldn't help it, and besides, he had warned him. Clay stared into the darkness. He couldn't see it, but he knew the city was out there. Not just the town, but also the city below. Right now that was easier to believe in than anything that might lay further up the mountain. As Clay pulled the other cord, the wooden blinds shut. His makeshift fortress was complete.

Clay lowered his head, his weary eyes drawn to the shiny silverware on a paper placemat that read "Acorn Diner". The knife and spoon reflected the colorful toothpicks overhead, specks of blue, green, yellow and red light dancing in the silver-plated utensils. The cheap silverware looked beautiful.

He wondered if he were to move it, at what point it would lose its reflection. Not one to leave well enough alone, he carefully picked up the knife, tilting it from side to side. But the colorful light glistened all the more. For each speck that would seemingly fall off the utensil's edge, another would appear to take its place.

Clay was mesmerized by the light, but rather than looking up, he stared deeper into the knife, tilting it forward, moving further into his fortress. Suddenly, the colorful lights vanished before his eyes, replaced by an elongated face trapped beneath water spots not previously noticed. Once again, he had gotten in the way. Holding the knife tighter, he stared at his distorted image. Whatever Heaven was trying to tell him, he wasn't getting the message.

As he lowered the knife, the waitress's face appeared in the blade.

"Coffee?"

Focusing on the silverware, he was careful not to make eye contact. "Please. I'm in a rush."

The waitress turned over the porcelain cup. "Do you know what you want?"

He raised his head above the propped up menu. It was another glimpse of Heaven.

All Clay saw were eyes. At first he didn't even realize they were hazel, just that they were bright, radiating warmth that overshadowed anything else in the room. Clay watched as the brightness was interrupted as she lowered her gaze to pour the coffee. He found himself waiting for her to look up again.

As she did, he lowered the menu. Maybe I do have time for a quick bite?

She smiled again, waiting for his response.

"Got any pastry?" Clay noticed her nametag as he stumbled over his words.

Becky pointed to the pastry case. It was loaded with cakes and pies. "What are you in the mood for?"

"What do you recommend?" He smiled, trying to muster up some charm.

"Tiramisu. It's our specialty."

"Italian or some California version?" Clay was suspicious. California had destroyed pizza with ham and pineapple. He didn't want to consider what it had done to Tiramisu.

"Well, our pastry chef is Italian, but he's also from California, so I don't know what to tell you."

"I'll take my chances." Clay was tempted to order more than dessert, but he had already stayed here too long. Reaching into his pocket, he searched for some change. "Do you have a phonebook? I need to call a cab."

"It's behind the counter. Help yourself."

Sliding out of the booth, Clay made his way to the counter. Aside from the waitresses, he was the only one not wearing black, which made him stand out all the more. He reached under the counter, retrieved the phonebook, and quickly returned to the privacy of his booth.

Becky brought the Tiramisu and set it in front of Clay before hurrying to respond to another customer.

He looked at it, puzzled. What the heck is that? Obviously, this was not Mike's Pastry. Clay took a bite, frowned, and then pushed it aside. Terrible. It was time to cut his losses and get out of this place. He reached for the phonebook. The Cliff Falls Yellow Pages had a glossy picture of the rushing falls on the cover. "Photoshop", he mumbled under his breath. He was doubtful that there were any falls in the town at all. It was probably just a clever marketing ploy some city manager came up with long ago to attract tourists.

Another wave of mourners arrived, settling into the booth behind Clay.

As he flipped through the pages, he couldn't help overhearing their conversation.

"Does Ted remind you of Al Gore? He's so stiff, like a robot."

Someone else laughed.

"When the old man goes, I don't know how that place can survive."

"Right or wrong, Reagan is the main attraction."

"I'm so glad Reagan did the eulogy."

Clay hated gossip, having been the object of it his whole life. He prided himself on never listening to it, whether it was about himself or someone else. Turning the page, he spotted an advertisement for a taxi company.

"You know my daughter works at the hospital. Apparently, after Rose died Reagan just up and disappeared. Ted was livid. He couldn't find Reagan anywhere."

Grasping the phonebook, Clay leaned back in spite of himself. He couldn't help but listen.

"That's why the funeral was tonight. They waited as long as they could. They almost had to hold it without Reagan."

Clay's jaw dropped, his body inching down the booth.

"I heard the same thing from some of the elders. He just disappeared."

As Clay slid down the booth, his eyes rose until they were staring at the gleaming toothpicks overhead.

"Wherever he went, it must have been important."

✳

Reagan buttoned his pajamas, staring at the untouched bed. She insisted on making it before leaving for the hospital. That was how Rose was. She even laid out his clothes for the next day. The matching shirt and tie were still resting on the perfectly folded quilt that was draped over the bed's edge. For forty-three years, he had slept beside her. Forty-three years. He told himself that once the funeral was over, then he'd be ready to sleep in it again. "The things we tell ourselves." Reaching for his bathrobe, he made his way into his study.

Downstairs, the kitchen was filled with casseroles. No doubt they started arriving the night he left, along with a steady stream of comforting widows eager to be first in line. Reagan knew the drill. He had witnessed this ritual countless times, always vowing that he would never be on the receiving end. Luckily, he wasn't, at least not initially. For all the problems his disappearance had caused, that was one benefit he was grateful for.

He had cleaned out his personal rainy day fund to pay for the third of Clay's debt that the court required. Now that it was raining in Reagan's own life, the money was useless anyhow.

Settling into his recliner in the study, he utilized his bathrobe as a blanket. Reagan stared at a picture of Rose on the nearby desk. It was the same one used on the cover of the funeral program. He was glad Ted had chosen it. It was Reagan's favorite, although he couldn't remember where it was taken. But the place did not matter, nor the lavender dress that she was wearing. It was her eyes. Everything you needed to know about Rose, you could find there. And they were never clearer, except that last night.

*"You're holding him back. Ted will never be a man until you let him fail and learn to pick himself up."*

*"Don't you worry about any of that now—"*

*"The one I'm worried about is you. When I'm gone who is going to comfort the 'Comforter in Chief'?"*

*Resting her eyes, the medication began taking effect. "Nobody escapes life."*

*Reagan recognized himself on the television.*

*"What is it?" Rose said, struggling to stay awake.*

*"They found him. Clay. After all these years."*

*Rose opened her eyes and focused on what was a blurry photograph of a man completely covered in flour. "If I was able, I would fly there and help the boy myself."*

"I believe you would," Reagan said as the memory faded. "I believe you would."

Reagan pulled the bathrobe tighter under his neck, wondering if he could make good on either promise. He fell asleep in the recliner, gazing at the silver-framed picture of Rose.

✳

Breathless, Clay returned to the church on foot and found the parking lot empty. All the cars were gone now. The only evidence of what had occurred were a few discarded programs with Rose's portrait on the cover scattered on the gravel pavement. Her knowing eyes welcomed him back.

His first instinct was to gather the programs and place them somewhere, anywhere else. But somehow he felt it was a greater sign of respect to leave them there, undisturbed. Some things, he reasoned, should not be so easily forgotten.

Crouching down, he picked one up for himself, noting the date. August 16th. She died on my birthday.

Turning his attention back up the hill, he made his way along the steep path, the sound of his breath breaking the night's silence. Approaching the crest, he hesitated, somehow surprised by the darkness that met him. The church's own fixtures were on a timer and were off for the night. It was almost as if the church were sleeping, resting for what would come in the morning.

Grasping the handle to the outside sanctuary doors, Clay rattled it, but found it locked. This time he was literally left out in the cold. Even if he weren't too tired to walk back to town, he knew that it was too late to find lodging for the night. He had to find another way. That's when his survival instincts kicked in.

Making his way around the perimeter of the church, he spotted a storage shed. Perhaps there's a tarp or something I can use as a blanket? He tried to open it, and to his amazement, not only was it unlocked, but a folded blanket with a new package of beef jerky sat waiting on the shelf. He smiled, grateful for the fool who forgot to lock it.

Clay settled onto a bench next to the church steps. He gnawed on the beef jerky and rummaged through his luggage. After putting on an extra sweatshirt and sweats over his jeans, he was still cold. He put on another two shirts, pulled his knit hat below his ears, and bundled up in the blanket. Leaning back, he rested his head on his duffel bag, which doubled as a pillow.

The sky was clear, each star fixed into position like an obvious map he could never decipher. He gazed upon the sky's majesty, realizing how only an hour before he would have settled for cellophane toothpicks lodged in a ceiling.

For a moment he felt like he was right where he was supposed to be. Despite everything that had or would happen, this night he was supposed to be here, on this bench, under this sky. That much he knew. With his head nestled on his duffel bag, Clay Grant fell asleep under the watchful stars.

✳

Deep in an alley in the North End, there was a quiet rumbling inside a dumpster. Burt Cummings sorted through the discarded documents, the shredded scraps, from the Boston Courthouse, searching for a lead before someone else found one. There was no way he was giving up now. He was enraged at himself for letting Clay slip through his fingers. Now everyone was looking for his cash cow! And after he had done all the legwork! Burt banged his fist against the inside wall of the dumpster. Who kept the pressure on Clay all those years, ensuring that they got the best performance out of him? Who held him accountable?

He told himself to be patient. He knew how Clay operated. There was no way he disappeared without leaving a trail. Under the cover of darkness, Burt dug through the mound of scraps and waste, determined to find what he was looking for.

## Chapter Nineteen

With heavy eyelids, Clay resisted the first signs of morning. The sun braised the side of his face, cutting the chill that enveloped the rest of his body. It had been a cold night and he wasn't yet thawed. A cool breeze swept over him. He was unsure where he was, like a traveling salesman who forgot what city he was in. He felt wooden planks under his back. Tell me I'm not drifting at sea? All the more reason to sleep in. As the rays intensified, he rolled over on the bench, his ears attuned to the rapid hissing of sprinklers in the distance. It was a gentle alarm clock allowing him to awake at his own pace.

As Diego Marquez stepped out of his flatbed truck, he spotted a man asleep on the bench. Always the first on property, he was used to discovering stranded travelers. Not too many homeless, the church was too removed for that. Hikers who misjudged the distance between the Peninsula and Half Moon Bay would occasionally set up camp for the night. They seemed to stumble upon the church just when they were too exhausted or lost to continue. The church was well positioned for just this event. However, for liability reasons, he was supposed to move them along.

As Diego shut the door, he saw the familiar blanket on the ground. He was glad this traveler found it. He knew the nights could get pretty cold, so he always kept one in the storage shed on the south side of the church for them to find, along with a snack, usually beef jerky. The staff was not always comfortable with their "overnight guests", but Diego had a soft spot for wanderers. At thirty years of age, he felt a church caretaker should do more than just set up chairs and maintain the grounds. Reaching into his truck, he retrieved a plaid thermos and approached the bench.

"Welcome to Hotel High Hope," Diego said, careful not to startle the man.

Clay reluctantly opened one eye as an Aztec face came into focus. The guy looked angelic with the sun at his back, his muscular build only undermined by the sparkle in his eye. Clay squinted as the sun emerged through the golden oak leaves overhead. It was all coming back to him now.

"I hate to tell you this, but you're in the line of fire." Diego pointed to the opposite end of the bench.

Clay raised his head only to discover his jeans were soaked from an over-reaching sprinkler. Plopping his head back onto the bench, he squeezed his eyes as the Rain Bird drenched his lower half.

"Some coffee will warm you up," Diego assured him, holding out the thermos. Twisting off the top, which doubled as a cup, he opened the container. The burnt aroma smelled like the inside of a donut shop.

Clay half expected an apple fritter. Stretching out his arms, he let out a discomforting yawn as he attempted to straighten his spine. "Maybe you should pour it on my back?"

Diego laughed, filling the plastic cup. "It's not gourmet, but it will do the trick."

"Are you sure there's enough?"

"There's plenty." Smiling, Diego handed him the cup.

Clay lazily sat up, making an effort to remove himself from the sprinkler's reach. Sipping the coffee, he stared at his surroundings. This was the first time he was seeing it in the daytime. It all looked too perfect. The mountainous scenery was beautiful. The vast landscape basked in the morning light, while the towering trees provided patches of protective shade along the rolling hillside. Everything was greener and more rustic than he had imagined. He stared at this new world, wondering if it would last or if it would come to an end as abruptly as everything else he had known.

"Just passing through?"

"I don't know." It was as truthful an answer as he could give. Nursing the coffee, he heard the crunching of tires on gravel. The sound overshadowed the hissing sprinklers.

"That's the boss."

Clay saw an SUV pulling into the upper parking lot.

"Don't worry. I'll take care of this." Diego handed him the thermos and approached the vehicle.

Reagan opened the car door, hesitating the way a man hesitates on the side of the bed in the morning. This would be his last hesitation for the day. He knew he couldn't afford another, not if he was going to hold the church together. In a few hours he would face everything he had set in motion and was doubtful he would have much to show for it. But Reagan was resilient. He always found a way.

"Didn't think you were coming in today," Diego said. He was usually the one to ask the direct question everyone else skirted. It was just his way. And without agenda. Most of the staff would never say the obvious, partially out of respect, partially out of self-interest. Diego figured honesty was the best form of respect.

"If I didn't get out of bed this morning, I might never," Reagan confided. Reaching for his briefcase, Reagan stepped out of the SUV, squinting as the emerging sun reflected off the car door. In the distance, he saw a disheveled man sitting on the bench.

"Don't worry about him," Diego said, "he was just..."

Reagan smiled as the sleepy-eyed rag-a-muffin came into focus. Clay Grant. Hope had arrived.

Yawning, Clay offered a tired wave.

Diego realized that they knew each other.

Reagan made his way across the lawn, his confident stride giving little indication of the grief he was carrying. Last night, Clay needed to know if this guy was alive. Now all he wanted to know was why Reagan flew 3,000 miles to help him right after his wife had died and what any of this had to do with him. But as Reagan drew closer, all those questions became less important. He saw the grief hidden in his eyes. Clay took off his knit hat and patted down his hair, embarrassed by his own tousled appearance.

Reagan stood before him beaming. "I knew you'd come."

Rising from the bench, Clay struggled to find the

appropriate words. Reaching into his back pocket, he retrieved the funeral program, holding it out in his hand. "I'm sorry."

Reagan glanced at the picture of Rose. "I know."

Clay didn't know what else to say, so he just waited, figuring Reagan would speak when he was ready. After a few moments he did.

"It was Rose who insisted that the church be built facing the city. If we were not going to be in the city we must at least face it, she reasoned. She was very fond of you."

Clay nodded, recalling the gift she had given him. In those days people were always giving "Little Guy Mike" gifts, usually with a more expensive motive included in the card. But this one was different. "She gave me that leather journal."

Reagan smiled, knowing it was a gesture typical of Rose.

"I remember looking at it disappointed, like 'What a crappy gift.' But that last summer, when everything went down, I found myself reaching for it more and more. I filled it cover to cover. I think I thought of her a little bit every time I wrote in it."

"She would be glad that you're here."

"Did you...?"

"It's in a safe spot."

"Thank you for everything, for the money and for trusting me to show up. That meant a lot."

"Well, as I said, I'm planning on putting you to work."

"Doing what?"

"We'll get to that."

"I'm not going to have to interact with people or anything like that, am I?"

"That's up to you."

Reagan noticed Ted's car pulling into the upper parking lot. Ted walked across the lawn, ignoring his father. He glanced at Clay, but didn't recognize him. Taking a few more steps, he hesitated, and then moved on.

Clay looked at Reagan to see if Ted knew. Reagan shook his head no.

"So what happens now?"

"Diego is going to show you your new home."

*

Diego unlocked the door to the studio loft. It was one of the few on campus and was tucked away in the back of the property above an old meeting room that pre-dated every structure except the old barn. It was a place of solitude, a writer's retreat where Reagan composed his earlier sermons and that first book that gained him national attention. But that was years ago. For the past two decades, it was residence to a steady stream of pastors and interns who were given housing in exchange for reduced compensation. Lately, it sat empty.

"It's small but has all the basics."

As the door opened, Clay hoped for something more than that saltbox in Boston with its porthole for a window. He wasn't disappointed.

Natural light filled the space, gleaming through the large window and off the hardwood floors. Tossing his duffel bag and backpack onto the twin bed, he briefly noted the night stand with an alarm clock that flashed 12:00 a.m. and a simple desk that sat beneath a vast window looking out over the hillside.

Clay moved to the window. The landscape was breathtaking, void of any man-made structures. At the base of the hillside, he could see a flowing brook, apparently originating from the elusive falls. Everything was starting to feel a little too good to be true.

"Good luck with that TV."

Clay turned. The light shined on the bulging glass. The old Zenith had seen better days. It was a relic from another era. Pliers rested on the wooden veneer, a necessity if you wanted to change the channel. It sat on a television stand with rabbit ears covered in aluminum foil.

Diego took hold of the antenna. "Cliff Falls, the heart of the technology revolution, but we still can't get decent reception. We're supposed to wire it for cable, but it keeps getting cut from the budget."

"It's perfect," Clay said with holy reverence.

"The college pastor lived here. After the tech bust the church let a lot of staff go. The Peninsula still hasn't recovered. Are you a pastor?"

"Me?" Clay chuckled. He had been mistaken for many things in life, but a pastor was never one of them. "No. I'm not a pastor."

Before Diego could ask another question, Clay changed the subject. "So are there *really* falls in Cliff Falls?"

Diego nodded yes. Moving to the window, he pointed. "Can you see that babbling brook down there?"

"Those are the falls?"

Diego laughed. "That's just an offshoot. The falls are further up the mountain. It's amazing how those powerful waters become a gentle brook by the time they make their way down here."

Clay leaned in, "Are you sure there isn't some guy up there flipping on a switch?"

"Depending on your theology, yes and no," Diego said smiling. "Believe me, they are breathtaking."

"How do you get to the falls?"

"I could tell you, but you'd probably get lost."

"Huh?"

Diego tried to explain. "There used to be trail markers that a bunch of Boy Scouts carved years ago. They weren't fancy but they were cut in the shape of an arrow and, if you were looking for them, they basically got you there and back."

"What happened to them?"

"Well, the arrows are still there. You just don't know it," Diego said.

Clay was confused.

"As part of a beautification project, some committee decided to plant indigenous flowers around the arrows to make them more appealing. When the shrubs matured, they grew over the arrows. Now you could stare at them all day long and not know they're pointing somewhere. Don't get me wrong. The flowers are beautiful. Tourists love to pose and take pictures in front of them. Unfortunately, they still get lost."

"So how do you find the falls?"

"The truth is you have to wander a bit. Wander and listen for them."

"Wandering is something I'm good at. Listening, not so much..."

Clay looked down at his wet jeans from the sprinkler. "What time did Reagan say to meet him in his office again?"

"9:30 sharp. It's in the administration building by the sanctuary. There are fresh towels in the closet." Diego checked his watch as he moved to the door. "If you hurry, you have time to take a hot shower," he said as he left.

Clay sat on the side of the bed and removed his shoes and wet socks as the shower heated up. He pressed his bare feet on the colorful oval rug. It had seen some wear but its muted colors were vibrant enough to be welcoming and useful at the same time.

Undressing, he placed his dirty clothes in a pile on the floor. He stepped into the shower, knowing that he would have to be quick if he were going to be on time. The heat was stinging, penetrating the pressure in his back. He scrubbed, trying his best to wash away the events of the past week. As the memories flooded back, Clay turned his face towards the powerful stream of water, forcing the thoughts from his mind.

Reaching for a towel, he placed it around his waist. Steam filled the bathroom, fogging up the medicine cabinet mirror above the vanity. With a washcloth, he wiped the mirror, catching a glimpse of his face before the steam returned to obscure his reflection. He tried again, but each time, the steam returned.

Clay opened the bathroom door and stepped into the living area. The steam poured out, traveling like breath across the room. Unzipping his bag, he searched for some clean clothes. Most of what he brought with him, he had worn the night before to keep warm. As he removed a shirt, he noticed the steam fogging up the vast window.

He sat on the side of his bed and felt something beneath. Reaching under the mattress, he removed his journal, and stared at the charred cover. Cradling it in his hand, he stood up.

Moving toward the window, Clay was curious if he would still be able to see the brook at the base of the hillside. As he looked into the glass, he saw the brook flowing through his reflection.

✳

The message went out, catching everyone off guard. The staff spilled out of cubes and private offices on the way to the conference room.

Alexis walked at a brisk pace down the corridor. Maggie, college intern and recent graduate of nearby Stanford University, trailed behind, busying herself with her Palm Pilot.

"Reagan's really here?" Max said with disbelief, emerging from his office dressed in obnoxious golfing attire. He was already on the course when he got the news.

"He's been in since seven," Alexis said.

"Ted, too?"

"Ted, too," Alexis replied.

"Unbelievable!" Max pulled out his cell, leaving a voicemail. "Reagan came in after all. You'll have to play without me."

Thomas, the church's Worship Director, stumbled out of his office wearing a brown sport coat as he joined the group down the corridor. "Who comes to work the day after his wife's funeral?"

"His behavior hasn't exactly been predictable lately," Paul, the Missions Pastor, said.

"Lately...?" Monica said rolling her eyes. "The kids in my Children's Ministry are more sensible."

Alexis shot Monica a look to keep her in line. "The man just lost his wife."

"You're the shrink, Alexis. It's too early for him to come back to work. Didn't you advise him against it?" Max said.

"Deaf ears."

"Alexis said Reagan has an important announcement to make," Maggie said, looking up from her Palm Pilot.

Thomas spoke up, "Maybe he's going to tell us where he went?"

*

Clay emerged from the loft with wet hair and a half-buttoned shirt. It was flannel and the only one he had left. He was clean now, almost presentable. Unfortunately, he was also late.

Rushing down the steps, he ran through the rustic campus picking up speed, his feet pounding the dirt path. The air was invigorating.

Usually he was running from something. Only now did he consider what he was running to. He tried to imagine what he'd be doing, what he had to offer, or to what extent he'd have to interact with others. If he had his choice he'd be out in the fresh air working with Diego in the garden, getting his hands dirty. Maybe I can fit in here? He felt a pebble lodged in his shoe. Instead of stopping, he raced on, determined to ignore the repetitive sting in his heel.

Diego and a crew were busy planting rose bushes in the new garden Reagan had commissioned a few months ago. Set apart behind a whimsical iron gate, it had only been installed a few days earlier. It was a muddy mess. The flowerless bushes were all thorns and twisted stems covered in fresh dirt. Reaching for the hose, he spotted Clay coming down the hill.

"You're late!" Diego shouted.

"I know! I know!" Clay shouted back.

"The church office is that way!" Diego pointed the hose in the other direction.

"Thank you!" Clay shouted, changing course.

Diego shook his head, amused by this latest addition to the church. Turning on the hose, he watered the shrubs, washing the fresh dirt off the memorial headstone: "Rose Irene Mitchell," carved in granite.

In the lower parking lot, Becky managed the tray of cranberry coffee cake as she shut the door to her Honda with her foot. It was still warm, steam trapped beneath the protective cellophane, with a note that read "High Hope/Staff Meeting—ASAP!" One of these days she was going to get access to the upper lot. The Acorn had assumed the meeting was cancelled, so they were caught off-guard when the church called it in. Luckily, a tray was just coming out of the oven. Becky volunteered to run it up, just as she had volunteered to work the night before when everyone else was at the funeral. As the new hire, she preferred to volunteer rather than be told what to do, especially when she knew she'd end up doing a particular task anyway. Until she gained seniority, it was part of the job, and besides, volunteering made her popular with the other waitresses. She learned early on that those relationships were ultimately more important than fighting over something she could just as easily get done.

Becky made her way up the hill. The truth was she didn't mind deliveries, except when they took her away from the peak times when she made her best tips. The morning rush could be the difference between covering rent and affording those simple extras, like flowers and trips to the nail salon, that made her feel a little pampered. She was surprised how important those little luxuries had become to her during the last year. Somehow they gave her the ability to deal with life's more mundane tasks, like carrying a tray of coffee cake up a sloping hillside. Nearing the crest, she forged ahead.

Picking up speed, she cut across the expansive lawn, determined to make it back before the end of the rush. The two-story building was just beyond the sanctuary. As she turned the corner, she looked up and saw a familiar face running straight towards her. As their eyes met, a collision seemed unavoidable. Becky gripped the tray of coffee cake in fear, her fingers tightening on the metal rim....

## *Chapter Twenty*

Shifting his weight in a split-second reaction, Clay flew head over heels into the bushes, tossing and tumbling. The branches absorbed the impact. Finally, he landed on his back as the dust kicked up.

"Are you all right?"

Standing over him were the same beautiful eyes from the night before. They stared at him with a look of concern.

"I'm fine... fine..." he coughed as the dust settled. "I think?" Trying to save face, he rolled out of the bushes and onto his feet. Clay dusted off his pants and picked leaves from his flannel shirt. He was no longer clean. He now resembled a kid who had spent the day playing in the woods.

"Do you always run that fast?"

"I was on my way to the church office—"

"Wait, I know you."

Clay froze, fearing she recognized him as "Little Guy Mike".

"You're the Tiramisu guy from last night."

Clay pulled twigs out of his hair, grateful she remembered him but unsure that he wanted to be associated with that Tiramisu.

"I thought you were just passing through?"

"As it turns out, I've decided to stay..." he said regaining his composure, "...at least a little while longer."

"I'm Becky."

"Nice to meet you, Becky." He looked into her eyes slowly, deliberately, and held her gaze until she glanced away. Usually he wouldn't use his real name in a new place, but Reagan let it slip when he met Diego. "I'm Clay."

"Look, I'm usually not this forward," Becky said, "but I really have to get back to work and..."

"No, really, I appreciate women who take initiative." His confident tone bordered cockiness.

"You do?"

"I'm flattered." He put the palm of his hand on his chest in an attempt to seem modest.

"About the coffee cake?"

"Huh?"

"Coffee cake." She looked down at the tray and then at him. "You're going to the church office, right? I thought you could take it with you."

"Of course, coffee cake," he said, pointing to the tray trying to save face.

"If it's a problem...?"

"I'd be glad, flattered actually, to deliver it for you."

"Way to help a girl out." Becky smiled, handing him the tray.

As she walked away, Clay was left holding the coffee cake.

✳

The staff spilled into the conference room, taking their usual seats around the oval table. It was on the second floor, just down the hall from Reagan and Ted's offices. A bay window looked out over the property. Although the sun's reflection off the wood paneling could be distracting, the staff preferred to keep the blinds open so that they could gaze out to the rolling hillside when staff meetings went long. This day, all eyes were on Reagan.

Glancing at the clock, Reagan addressed the staff. "She was the heartbeat of this church and she thought so much of each of you."

Sipping coffee around the table, the staff listened intently. Reagan could see the loss of Rose visible in their eyes, too. She and he had handpicked them for their ability and loyalty. The ministries they ran were mini-churches within the larger body, places where people got spiritually fed and felt a sense of community.

He knew what they were thinking. They needed to know that he could recover from this loss and continue to lead. Not just for their sake but also for the people they served. He could mourn on his own time. He had a job to do now.

"Many of you are aware that I took some time off. I needed that. But now I'm back, ready to move this ministry, the ministry that Rose loved, forward."

Reagan had to hold the church together, especially since the tech bust. The church had been enduring an ongoing financial crisis; everyone was feeling the pinch and everything was accomplished on the leanest of budgets. Although the church was forty-years-old, it felt like a startup without adequate funding, re-inventing itself at every turn in hopes of staying relevant.

As he went on, Ted quietly slipped into the room, taking his seat beside his father.

"One thing we know about family is that they stick together, especially in challenging times."

I can't listen to this, Ted said to himself. He tuned his father out and turned his thoughts to the sermon he was scheduled to give this Sunday. Ted only got to preach a few times a year, usually when his father was traveling. Or on obscure dates like the Sunday after Christmas or, in this case, the Sunday after his mother's funeral. Although he was barely speaking to his father, he assumed it was still a go, especially since he had to scrap the eulogy he had written. As a rule they never announced when Ted preached for fear it would affect attendance. Ted wished they would. He would rather preach to an empty church than deal with a packed house that had just been informed that an understudy would now be playing the lead role. For years he waited in the wings, believing that if his father just put his full confidence behind him, he would have a shot at the church embracing him. Don't hold your breath.

"God has hidden gifts in our hearts, gifts we may not even know we have or see in each other. Rose always believed in you. We must be a family that believes in each other."

"Where's he going with this?" Thomas whispered to Max.

"Somewhere," Max whispered back. "Just wait..."

"As of Sunday, Ted will be taking a more active role. It's

time to think about succession."

Alexis spoke up. "You're retiring?"

Ted looked up in disbelief, questioning if he had heard his father correctly.

The staff's contained expressions said it all. Reagan knew that they couldn't voice their concerns with Ted present. And that's why he didn't make the announcement until Ted arrived.

"I'm not retiring, but I'm not going to live forever. I will continue on as Founding Pastor."

Ted stared at his father. Was this really happening?

Reagan caught Alexis' eye. She knew what that meant.

"We're very happy for you," Alexis said, leading the staff in offering obligatory congratulations.

"Thank you," Ted said awkwardly.

As she clapped, the rest of the room joined in.

"Well, at least the surprises are out of the way," Max interjected to break the awkwardness of the moment.

As if on cue, Clay appeared in the doorway with the coffee cake, hair tousled, twigs on his shirt and his pants dirt-stained.

Reagan shot him a cautionary glance.

"I'm just dropping this off," Clay said. He put the tray on the table and made a quick exit.

"Wait in the office next door. I'll be with you shortly," Reagan said.

"He's meeting with the new delivery guy?" Max said under his breath.

Ted cocked his head.

# Chapter Twenty-One

Clay sat restless in a chair, fingers tapping on the desk.
He had that awful feeling he used to get whenever he was
summoned to a studio executive's office. And that never
ended well. Sometimes it was to inform him that there was a
change in plans, always something he never had control over,
like writing his best friend off the show. More often it was to
clarify expectations and why he was suddenly the root of the
problem at hand. As a kid, he didn't know any better. He'd just
sit there and take it.

He glanced around the room. It was neat and organized.
Every book and pencil was in its proper place. If it were his
office, he would turn the desk around so it faced the window.
Why face a hallway when you could look out over that
landscape?

His eye caught a glimpse of a picture in a silver frame
on the desk. It was of Ted, his wife and son, a happy family.
Probably their Christmas card. He picked it up thinking about

Tyler from the night before.

"That was taken on Founder's Day."

Clay looked up, realizing that Ted had stepped into the office.

"It was all we could do to get my son to sit still long enough to take the picture." Ted smiled, shaking his head as he moved behind his desk. "He's a handful."

Clay glanced at the photograph again before placing the frame back on the desk. "I'm sorry about your mother's passing."

Ted stared out the window. "I'm managing. But my father has hardly been himself."

Clay turned his head, keeping an eye on the door. "Where is your father?"

"I don't know," Ted said with sarcasm. "He slipped out of staff meeting before I could speak with him."

"Maybe I'll come back?" Clay nervously rose from the chair.

"Look, I know who you are." Ted stared right at him. "You look different but you haven't changed."

Clay sunk back into his seat. This was going to get ugly.

"What are you doing here? This is a church not a hideout."

"Hey, this was your father's idea, not mine."

"My father is a visionary, thinks outside the box. Sometimes too outside the box." Ted had just won his father's confidence. He wasn't about to jeopardize the church. "It's not right for you to bring your mess here."

"My mess?"

"You're more famous for your messes than your TV show!"

"You know more about my life than I do? I never took you for one who reads the tabloids."

"They were in the hospital waiting room."

"You need to talk to Reagan about this." Clay stood up to leave.

"Why him?" Ted's face was red and his voice was getting louder. "Of all the people in the world, what made you track down my father after all these years?"

Clay wasn't twelve anymore and wasn't about to take much more. "I told you. You need to talk to your father about this."

"My mother dies and you show up on his doorstep? Don't you have a conscience?"

"He tracked me down."

"That's impossible. When would he have?" Ted's eyes widened. Slowly, he realized what his father had done. Ted felt the abandonment all over again. His relationship with his father was just one more thing he tried to hold together that had long since been broken.

"He showed up in Boston a few days ago. Before I knew it, he spoke to the judge, worked out a deal to pay off my debt. I didn't ask for a dime. He did that all on his own."

Ted was furious. "We're paying off your debt? Do you know how cash strapped this church is? I swear. You child stars are all alike."

"Hey, wait a minute. The deal is that I would work it off."

"Doing what? What could you possibly do here to pay that off? From what I read, that's a big debt. How long are you planning on being here?"

"I don't know. Everything's happened pretty fast. I just figured that stuff would work itself out."

"Here's some free advice, before you enter into a deal with

my father, it's always a good idea to look closely at the terms."

Clay and Ted realized that Tyler was standing in the doorway. The boy was disheveled like Clay, hair ruffled, covered in dirt but with a note pinned to his shirt. Tyler recognized Clay from the night before. "Are you in trouble, too?"

"Oh, yeah."

Ted realized that they knew each other. He unpinned the note from Tyler's teacher and glanced over it. "Wait here! I'll deal with you later. I have to talk to your grandfather right now."

Tyler let out an impressive laugh once his father stepped out of the office. "Whatever you did, it must have been big."

"Does your dad always get that worked up?"

"He's been worse since my mom left for grad school." Tyler made a fist and punched Clay in the arm. "Don't worry about it."

Clay slouched in his chair.

"Are you hungry?"

Clay's eyes widened. "Starving. I didn't even get any coffee cake."

"Follow me." Tyler offered a mischievous smile.

"Aren't you supposed to wait?"

Clay followed Tyler through the corridor and down the back stairs. As they made their way outside the administration building, Tyler made sure that the coast was clear before cutting across the expansive lawn.

"Come on." Tyler darted ahead, taking cover behind a protective tree.

Clay tried to keep up. Catching his breath, he turned his

head and looked back. Through a vast tree branch, he could see a view of Reagan's office window. Reagan was trying to calm Ted down. Both were engaged, standing face to face. After a moment of the heated exchange, Ted turned away from his father and Reagan put his hand on Ted's shoulder, as if conceding. Clay knew what that meant. Reagan was forced to choose Ted over him. And that's the end of my new beginning.

"Are you coming or not?" Tyler called out, reaching for the asthma inhaler in his pocket.

Taking a last look at the window, Clay continued on.

∗

The church kitchen was a heavily guarded fortress. Not only did it have a security camera outside, but also because of its proximity to Friendship Courtyard, it was virtually impossible to enter without being noticed. The only other way in, though quite unlikely, was through the service window in Celebration Hall. Even then the intruder would have to have stolen a key to the service window and then have been small enough to slip through before opening the swinging door to any accomplices. The staff quickly dismissed this unlikely scenario, but mysterious food raids continued to baffle them.

"Are you sure we're allowed in here?" Clay said.

Tyler's feet dangled in the air as he squeezed through the opening. "You worry too much."

"I just don't want to get you into trouble."

"I'm a PK. I'm supposed to get into trouble."

"What's a PK?" Clay heard a loud thump as Tyler landed in

the kitchen.

"A preacher's kid!" Tyler rumbled through the kitchen, bumping into pots and pans. "I got a reputation to live up to." And as easy as that, the door swung open.

The inside of the kitchen smelled like ice burn and Orange Tang. Black rubber mats covered the floor, while stainless steel refrigerators, complete with padlocks, lined the walls.

Clay smirked as Tyler removed a key ring from his pocket and began trying various keys. This kid was too much. After a moment, the locks started popping open.

"Jackpot!"

With all this security, Clay half expected to discover the Ark of the Covenant. Or at the least a fatted calf chained inside. He rolled his eyes. He just couldn't imagine what sacred grub was worth protecting until visions of prosciutto and prime rib began dancing in his head. Stomach growling, he waited in anticipation.

One by one, the three refrigerators opened. "What will it be?"

Clay's hopeful eyes scanned the shelves. The multitude of leftovers sat in aluminum containers covered in plastic wrap. It looked like the day after Thanksgiving; actually, the day, after the day, after the day of Thanksgiving. Each tray was clearly labeled with a ministry name followed by an ominous warning that read: "Do Not Touch".

Tyler read off the labels as if they were the specials of the day. "Leftover pasta salad from the Women's Ministry, a few turkey burgers from the Singles' Ministry social, or maybe flank steak from the College Ministry's outreach?"

Clay was overwhelmed by the culinary selection, although

he had yet to see anything that merited being kept under lock and key.

"And if you don't like any of that?" Tyler unlocked the walk-in freezer. "There is always the High Hope favorite, PriceSmart lasagna!"

Frost poured out as he opened the industrial door. There was shelf after shelf of PriceSmart lasagna, probably fifty trays.

"That's a lot of lasagna," Clay said over the roaring hum of the freezer fan. "Is it any good?"

Tyler stared at Clay in disbelief. "You've never had PriceSmart lasagna?"

Clay shook his head no, somehow embarrassed by the admission.

"Sorry. I just assumed you were a Christian."

Clay grinned. "What does PriceSmart lasagna have to do with being a Christian?"

"Are you kidding me? It's like the official food of Christianity. It's the cheapest, easiest thing to serve. It's as common to church life as miniature golf, bowling, or renting *The Princess Bride.*"

"*The Princess Bride?*"

"No dirty language or naked people." Tyler closed the freezer door. "You can't imagine how much PriceSmart lasagna a Christian eats a year!"

"But is it any good?"

Tyler stopped in his tracks, having never considered the question. "It's the only lasagna I know."

"That's one of the saddest things I've ever heard."

"So what will it be?" Tyler started removing trays from the

refrigerators. "Personally, I'd take the flank steak."

Conviction came over Clay. As hungry as he was, he couldn't get past the "Do Not Touch" labels.

"We can't eat this. It's like stealing." Clay pointed to the names on the labels. "This food belongs to these ministries."

Tyler rolled his persuasive blue eyes. Obviously, Clay was only familiar with literal interpretations of the Bible. "And what are ministries supposed to do?"

For the life of him, Clay couldn't muster up an answer.

"Feed the poor! I don't know about you, but I'm broke."

Clay laughed as the miniature theologian removed the flank steak and placed it on the center counter top.

"Wait until dessert," Tyler said with excitement. "Alcoholics Anonymous makes killer oatmeal cookies!"

They sat on the stainless steel counter top that was covered with leftovers and open containers. Clay finished off another bowl of chili while Tyler munched on his fourth oatmeal cookie. They had pieced together a feast from all the scraps and the food coma was setting in.

"So what's so terrible about being a 'PK'?"

"You're joking, right? It's the worst." Tyler chewed on the cookie. "People are always coming up to me, pinching my cheeks, and telling me how cute I am. I hate that."

Clay scraped the bottom of the bowl with his spoon. "I wasn't a 'PK', but I can relate. By the time I was your age, I had no feeling left in my cheeks."

"And that's not the worst part. I have to be involved with everything. People are always staring at me. It's like they are waiting for me to mess up."

"Tell me about it." Clay licked the spoon, recalling his own youthful plight.

"You have no idea."

"Oh, you'd be surprised."

"And when I do get into trouble, the whole church knows about it. The whole church! Then everybody is either giving you advice or telling you how lucky you are." Tyler took a last look at the half-eaten cookie, tossing it back on the counter. "I don't feel lucky."

"That stinks," Clay empathized.

"My mom is always reminding dad and grandpa that I'm not 'church property'."

"But your dad was a 'PK'?"

"Grandpa says he's still waiting for dad to mess up."

"Trust me, you're better off not listening to what people say about you, good or bad."

"I get that."

"You do?"

"People project onto me their own desire for moral perfection," Tyler said nonchalantly, obviously repeating something he'd been told. "An unrealistic expectation I can't live up to. Ultimately, I mess up and they're disappointed."

Clay shot Tyler a "Did you just say that?" look.

"At least that's what my therapist says."

"Therapist? What are you, nine?"

"I'm a 'PK.' The sooner the better." Just as Tyler resigned himself to his fate, Diego entered the kitchen.

"Busted."

Tyler froze when he realized that Diego was in the doorway. He knew he was in trouble and that he couldn't outrun Diego.

Hopping off the counter, Clay attempted to take the blame. "It's my fault, really. I was hungry and the kid was just trying to help me out."

Diego smiled at Clay. "Nice try." He held out his hand in front of Tyler. "All right. Hand them over."

Reluctantly, Tyler reached into his pocket, pulling out Diego's key ring.

"You're getting too good at swiping these."

Clay made an appeal to Diego, trying to protect Tyler. "Is there any way we could prevent the kid from getting into trouble?"

"Don't worry about it." Diego glanced at Tyler. "This time!"

Tyler smiled. "You haven't told on me yet."

"The key word is 'yet'. Now clean this up!"

Tyler hopped off the counter and began wiping the surface, putting containers into the trash. He resembled a miniature custodian.

Diego turned to Clay. "Reagan is looking for you."

Clay rolled his eyes. He knew what that meant. He was convinced Reagan was going to break the deal. He hadn't been here twenty-four hours and the place was already turned upside down. That was almost a personal record.

Clay followed Diego outside the kitchen. They stopped in front of Friendship Courtyard.

Clay squinted from the sharp sunlight. "That's cool, the way you look out for Tyler."

"He's a good kid. Just has a lot of pressure on him."

"His mom isn't coming back, is she?"

Diego shook his head no.

After an awkward moment, Diego noticed that Clay looked a bit pale. "Man, you don't look so good."

Clay rubbed his stomach. "I just ate my weight in leftover chili from Volunteer Appreciation Day."

"Volunteer Appreciation Day? That was like six weeks ago."

Clay looked like he was going to be sick. "Tyler!"

Diego patted him on the back as they continued to walk. "Crime doesn't pay, my friend. Crime doesn't pay."

＊

Ted stood in the pulpit, practicing his sermon to an empty sanctuary. His tone and animated gestures were forced. Each time he said "Juanita Gonzalez" he used a Hispanic accent.

"You see Juanita Gonzalez had a fuel problem. But not the kind of fuel you're probably thinking of."

The next line fell flat. "Juanita Gonzalez was low not on food or gasoline, but faith." Ted tried again, this time using a signature Bill Clinton hand gesture, making a fist while pointing with his thumb. "Juanita Gonzalez was low not on food or gasoline," he paused, "but faith."

Reagan and Clay settled into the dusty theater seats in the balcony loft, secretly observing Ted's performance. They spoke in a quiet whisper so as not to be noticed.

"He's been over-coached. That's my fault."

Reagan turned to Clay. "This isn't inspiring you, is it?"

"If there really is a Juanita Gonzalez, Ted doesn't know her."

It sounded like one of those contrived campaign stories politicians tell to show that they're connected with the people. Clay learned early on to never underestimate your audience.

They can see right through it. Glancing at Reagan, he only wished he had been that perceptive. Like a fool, Clay had underestimated Reagan's ability to stick by him. What did he expect? Blood was thicker than water. Shifting uncomfortably in his seat, he waited for Reagan's rationale of why he was going to break the deal.

"I spoke to my generation. We hoped that Ted could speak to his."

Normally, Clay would show some restraint, but at this point he had nothing to lose. "Is the real problem the message or the man?"

"I always believed that the right words could change the man."

"Well, these *aren't* them. Not that I go to church. But if I had to sit through this every week, I don't think I'd come back. Ever."

"I agree. And that is why I've decided that the church is never going to hear it."

"What?" Clay was surprised by the admission.

"I've obtained someone to write it for him."

Clay smiled knowingly, familiar with the nameless ghostwriters who would come in to punch up a script. In the end, everything was show business. He felt foolish thinking Reagan was above such practices. He whispered back, "I hope he's good."

"I'm betting on it. In fact I've bet a great deal on it." Reagan turned to Clay and smiled.

It took a moment for Clay to catch on. "You have got to be kidding me! You brought me all the way here for this?" Clay felt the adrenaline race through his body.

"I thought that you and Ted could work together. I now realize that is not possible. So you will write it."

"I'm not a pastor!"

"Good. We have plenty of them."

"I don't write anymore, let alone anything that sounds like a sermon."

"Not a sermon, a message. It doesn't have to be too long. Just share a word that will resonate with the people, something that you would want to hear from the pulpit. That is all I am looking for, something you would want to hear."

"No one cares what I have to say. I was an actor, not a writer."

"I care. And I think our church would, too. I believe that you could really help Ted."

"This is insane. And, it's dishonest."

"Dishonest?" Reagan reached into his pocket and removed a crumpled paper. "I also spent some time with your lawyer when I was in Boston. It seems that he didn't write that compelling argument that impressed the judge after all. Clay, you wrote this. And you said it yourself."

*"When you look at Clay Grant, what are you looking for? Because that's exactly what you're going to find."*

Clay looked at the crumpled paper filled with his own handwriting.

"God has given you a gift with words. You need to use that gift. Think about it, even as a boy, whenever your life got tough, you wrote. That journal. Clay, you kept it after all these years."

Clay realized that Reagan was serious. Eyes rising, Clay stared at the jagged crack that skirted the central beam in the ceiling, waiting for the whole roof to cave in.

"What this church needs is the humanity of someone who has been broken, someone like you. I'll take the risk. I'd rather you try and fail than sit on the sidelines. You've sat on the sidelines too long." Reagan glanced at his son in the pulpit. "This church won't receive Ted's words, but they might receive yours."

*

Thunder rattled the windows of the motel lobby, the steady downpour beating against the glass. Burt waited for the airport shuttle.

Gossip magazines with headlines about Clay littered the counter. Burt tucked a few in his bag. He couldn't wait to get out of Boston. How the hell does someone disappear without leaving a trail? He entered his credit card into the airline website, booking a ticket to the one person he was sure could point him in the right direction.

Glancing out the rain-soaked window, he spotted newspapers for sale covering the story. Headlines were one thing. A photo was another. The first picture of Clay now could fetch up to three hundred thousand. Burt thought about the tattered photo of Clay that he kept in his wallet—the humiliation of the pose—and it spurred him on. He knew how to control that boy. There was no way he was going to let someone else find the real Clay first. Smiling, Burt was determined to outsmart Clay, the other paparazzi and press. The shuttle bus pulled up. Printing out his receipt, he knew exactly where he was headed.

*Chapter Twenty-Two*

Clay's first instinct was to run. As he returned to the loft to pack, he plotted his escape along the way. He'd borrow Diego's truck to get down the mountain, making sure to let him know where it was once he was out of sight. He knew he'd have to lay low for a while. The BART station in Daly City was probably his best bet. He had spotted it from the highway on the drive in. He could catch a train or bus there. He wouldn't care where it was headed as long as it was away from here. He felt manipulated. He knew he had every right to run. And that was exactly what he planned to do when he entered the loft. So why did his duffel bag and backpack both remain empty on the hardwood floor?

Lying on the bed, he stared at the ceiling, his thoughts churning. I can't understand it. What would make Reagan think I could write Ted's message? He thought about that crumpled piece of paper. He had stayed up half the night writing it, his ink-stained fingers cramping as he articulated a defense he had played out in his mind a thousand times before. In the end, it wasn't enough. He couldn't get past it. He had watched his lawyer throw it in the trash. So much of his heart had been poured into those words that it was as if a piece of him was being discarded, another fragment out there that he'd never get back. His eyes filled with water.

The idea that Reagan had retrieved it overwhelmed him. Clay couldn't bring himself to run out on the man, at least not yet.

There has to be another way. And then the idea came to him. He got up from the bed and moved to the window. He spotted the flowing stream at the base of the hill. Maybe it wasn't such a crazy idea after all?

Ted is at risk, not me. What's the worst that can happen? If it was a disaster, they'd send me packing anyhow. Ted would insist on it.

He wouldn't screw up on purpose, but the odds were in his favor. He didn't have to run out on Reagan. All he had to do was come up with something that let Reagan know he tried. Staring at that babbling creek, he wondered if he could find the words.

Clay walked across campus. He wasn't running. He was walking. There was a difference.

He couldn't believe that he was actually considering writing it, or that a part of him was flattered—the boy inside that was never heard. As a kid, it was a constant battle. As a teenager, it was just outright rebellion. He didn't have a say in anything. Even his interviews were well scripted. It was ironic: now that someone wanted to hear what he had to say, it would be said through someone else.

He thought about what Reagan said about the right words changing the man. All Clay knew were the words that had changed him, the accusing comments that kept him in line and replayed in his head. He prided himself on not caring what other people thought or said, but if he were honest, he knew that stuff lingered and had a way of resurfacing, especially when he was tired and alone. The wrong words stay with you a lot longer than the right ones. He wouldn't say it, but that was what he believed.

Continuing toward the center of campus, he took in the quiet majesty of the landscape. It was beautiful. He had to admit that was one promise Reagan came through on. That, and the bad television reception.

He thought about what he wanted to hear from the pulpit. Even if he could imagine what he would want to hear, he was certain it wasn't fit for public airing. One thing for sure, he thought as he continued down the hill, if he had any shot at helping Ted, he would have to keep all his private thoughts about the realities of life to himself.

✳

Alexis confronted Reagan as they made their way down the church corridor. Their conversation was as intense as their pace. Not wanting to be overheard, they spoke in quiet tones.

"Resigning?" Reagan said.

"You still have time to change this."

"Names. I need names."

Alexis was reluctant. As a therapist, she respected

confidentiality, but as a co-worker, her instinct was to prevent a mass exodus. "Paul. Monica."

Reagan didn't flinch. He expected casualties. "Is that it?"

Alexis hesitated before breaking the bad news. "And Max."

"Max?" Reagan was clearly disappointed. Every church has a leader that the people follow regardless of title or position. At High Hope, that was Max. In the three years he had been there, young families began returning to the church for the first time in more than a decade. "We can't afford to lose him."

"They've been sitting on offers for weeks. This announcement about Ted was the deciding factor."

They passed Monica Wilson in the corridor.

"Great staff meeting, Reagan. Very inspiring!" She held a thumb up to emphasize the point.

"Thank you for your belief, Monica." Reagan offered a confident grin as Monica moved down the corridor. "Offers from where?"

"Monica's going to Harvey Maxwell's church in Florida, and Paul, he's leaving the ministry. He was offered a job at Oracle."

"Oracle?" They stepped into Reagan's office. "It's one thing to lose a pastor to Harvey Maxwell, but to Larry Ellison?"

Alexis tried to explain. "His kids are almost in college. He thinks he can make good money."

"And Max?"

"Pearl Tree Pond."

Reagan shook his head in disappointment.

"That's where he went last month when he took those personal days," Alexis said. "I know their offer will be hard to beat."

"They're not letting him preach in the main service,

are they?"

"Maybe the Sunday after Christmas, that sort of thing."

"Max won't survive one winter in Chicago," Reagan said.

"You've taken away their reason to stay. You're betting everything on this succession plan."

\*

As Clay came down the hill, he stumbled upon the High Hope Bookstore situated in Friendship Courtyard, next to a vending cart that sold coffee and pastries. Hopefully, they'll have what I'm looking for.

The bookstore was really more of a gift shop than anything else, filled with keepsakes and collectibles. There were separate teen and children's sections and a special counter where you could buy taped sermons from the previous weeks. Although you could now get some of what they carried online, people still preferred to come into the store. The inspirational atmosphere was invigorating and made people feel as if they were embodying Reagan's message of hope. All this was especially true since word got out about Rose. It had been busy all week, but the store had yet to extend its hours. It was pretty much cleaned out. Anything with a High Hope logo went fast. Everyone, it seemed, wanted a piece of Hope.

The volunteers were anxious to ring up the last of the customers and close up shop by three. Bessie and Grace were sisters and knew if they hurried, they were usually able to catch the hourglass opening of their favorite soap opera, *Days of Our Lives*, on the old tabletop television set in the backroom. Although the reception was poor, the iconic theme was stirring enough to make them feel like they were listening to an old radio broadcast. If they missed the theme, they were never quite able to get into the rest of the show and would instead focus on the poor picture quality and unrealistic storylines, like when Marlena was possessed by the devil. Who believes these things?

So at a quarter to three, the sisters began giving subtle hints to the customers that they were closing, like turning off the soaring praise music and shutting down the rotating display cases. In fact, the closer it came to the three o'clock hour, the less inspiring everything seemed.

Needless to say, they were none-too-happy when Clay wandered in while everyone else was checking out.

Noticing their anxious smiles, Clay was distracted by the picked-over inspirational products scattered throughout. He was confident that if he got inside Ted's audience's mind, he could bust out something that was at least better than Ted's "Juanita Gonzalez" message.

Clay's eyes rose to the artwork for sale on the walls, scenes of quaint cottages with thatched roofs nestled in tranquil valleys, framed with comforting scriptures about peace and serenity. They weren't originals. They were "hand-numbered" prints that had been, according to the nearby sign, "individually highlighted by trained apprentices under the supervision of the artist". Staring at the cottages, Clay was curious who lived inside. He half-expected one of the three little pigs to come wandering out.

Making his way to the back of the store, he perused the book section. It was a monument to Reagan, his thirty titles proudly displayed. He picked up *The Road to Hope* and he flipped through the pages, fixated on the motivational sayings that were highlighted in bold text. They seemed more inspirational than theological, the sum of which was sort of a roadmap to a better life. It occurred to Clay that you didn't even need to read it; if you only read the chapter titles, you pretty much read the book. In fact, the title alongside Reagan's confident face was probably enough to lift your spirits if this were the sort of thing you bought into.

Maybe this stuff did work, as long as you lived in one of those quaint, thatched-roofed cottages in one of those villages featured in the paintings. And just as long as the mortgage was paid and the creditors weren't calling and you hadn't been informed that the government was going to build a new freeway through your front yard. Yeah, then this stuff might work.

But the only valleys Clay had known were anything but tranquil. Pits really, that were steep and incredibly hard to climb out of. He wasn't one for positive sentiments, the kind that disappear the moment you wander from your safe cottage, given you live in one in the first place. Even if he was just being cynical, he knew better than to lift his hopes that high.

As he stared at the book in his hand, he knew if this is what the audience wanted, he was uncertain he could deliver. There was only one Reagan Mitchell. Reagan could get away with this stuff, but not Ted.

Just when Clay felt that the situation was looking dim, the lights went out.

Bessie stood by the switch, smiling. It was the last of her not-so-subtle hints that it was closing time.

Message received. Tossing the book back onto the pile,

he turned to leave. It was then that he encountered Jesus, well sort of. His path was blocked by Grace, who held open an oversized "Jesus is my Shepherd" afghan to fold. Clay was taken aback at the sight of the overly friendly Savior in colorful woven thread towering over him. Jesus wasn't just smiling. He had perfect teeth. He looked like he was chosen to be Israel's new version of the *Bachelor.*

Pivoting away, Clay backed into a table displaying "Jesus" consumer products, knocking them over. Biblical action figures, Last Supper platters, "Jesus and the Boyz" T-shirts, and "Lamp unto my feet" night-lights tumbled off the shelves, crashing to the ground. The tinny sound of the Last Supper platters echoed throughout the store.

Bessie and Grace watched in dismay, their anxious smiles turning into frowns as all hope for their favorite soap opera quickly faded.

Clay felt bad that he had backed into the table, but it wasn't like he deliberately turned it over. Who would do that? Attempting to pick up the items that were scattered about, Clay recalled a time when his own face was plastered on cheap merchandise. Looking at the muscle-clad Jesus action figure in his hand, he knew Jesus must feel the same way.

"Bad licensing deals, huh?" Clay said knowingly to the Pro Wrestler Jesus with a gritty smile. "I know all about that. I bet you don't even get a cut? Me neither."

\*

Max stepped into Reagan's office. He was wearing Thomas' sport coat over his golfing attire. "Alexis said you wanted to see me?"

Reagan offered Max a seat. "My afternoon is packed, so I'll make this fast. As I see it, you have a problem on your hands."

"I have a problem?" Max grinned, curious where this was going.

Reagan reached into his desk and removed a golf ball. He held it between his thumb and index finger. "Maybe you've forgotten, but golf balls are white."

Max stared at the ball confused. "I don't follow."

"Golf balls are white. Unfortunately, so are golf courses, in Chicago. Not green. White. How are you going to see the white ball if the course is covered in snow?" Reagan tossed the ball to Max.

"Alexis told you—"

"Look, we both know that the point of any game is to never take your eye off the ball. I'm afraid that is exactly what you are doing."

"Ted is a good man but he's not you. Right or wrong, you're the reason people come week after week. You're the draw."

"We are building a new future here."

"This church is like an upside down pyramid. It's built on you."

"I'm not disappearing. I'm just giving Ted an opportunity."

"It's not just about Ted," Max said. "Every year we are going 'in an exciting new direction.' Never getting to the middle of the last vision before we start the next one. Chasing what successful megachurches are doing, trying to be *relevant*."

Reagan was clear. "I don't want to be relevant anymore. I want to be..."

Max held up his hand. "Please don't say *real* or *authentic*.

I am so tired of those buzz words. And whatever you want us to be, Ted can't do it. He's not you. The audience you've built doesn't want him. They want a star. So unless you have one of those up your sleeve—"

Reagan grinned. "Your future is here. You need to rethink this."

"I have to look out for my family. If this place unravels—"

"You're not leaving."

Max let out a chuckle. "I admit it. Reagan Mitchell can motivate anyone to do just about anything. But not me. Not this time."

"Paul and Monica are leaving," Reagan admitted.

"I know."

"I won't try to stop them," Reagan said. "Their hearts left long ago. But not you. Your heart is in the soil of this church."

"Don't do this."

"Think of all the families that are invested here because of you. Picture their faces. They're still young in their faith. You're going to walk out on them now?"

Max grasped the golf ball tighter.

"Pearl Street Pond is a turn-key operation. You'll never be able to do there what you can accomplish here." Reagan made a final appeal. "Don't take your eye off the ball. Not now."

# Chapter Twenty-Three

Kicking up dirt with each step, Clay made his way into town along Ridge Road, descending the tree-lined hill. He had heard of determined men walking across the country on foot, but until this moment, he had never fully understood it. If not for the media attention it would surely attract, or what lay on the other side of the country for him, namely Boston, he might have kept walking.

He felt caught between what had been stirred up inside of him and the danger that lay further down the mountain. It had been a heavy news cycle but by now the mainstream media would be all over the story. Burt would be more determined than ever, wanting to profit from the story before the paparazzi did. The outside world wasn't safe, and yet something about seeing all those cheap consumer products in the High Hope Bookstore made him want to flee.

Slowing his pace, he approached the quaint town. Calm down. Shake it off. But that was easier said than done. Memories could be as powerful as the words that accompanied them; both capable of erasing the distance time had put in place.

Rounding the Acorn Diner, he stepped from the dirt road onto the steady pavement of Cliff Falls Drive. Clay glanced into the window, hoping a glimpse of Becky might brighten his day. Instead, Ted sat at the counter. Cringing, he stepped away from the glass before Ted could see him, curious what language could make this guy appealing. Ted was not worth the aggravation but Clay knew he didn't have much of a choice. He had to buy time until things blew over. But he wasn't doing this for Ted. He was doing it for Reagan.

Continuing down the street, he passed the various storefronts in the picture-perfect town: Nancy's Knitting Shop, Cliff Falls Hardware Store, Magnificent Music Shoppe, and The Perfect Note Stationery Store. He felt foolish getting so worked up but didn't think he should have to feel that junk again just to please an audience. That's the life he ran from. He hated being in that position.

Clay hesitated in front of the firehouse. Why am I making this so difficult? Keep it simple. Show you tried. That will buy you time until things settle down and allow you to save face with Reagan. That's what he reminded himself as he stood in the town square, hoping that his bare minimum would be enough. Now if he could just figure out how to write something that pleased the High Hope audience and didn't make him stir up bad memories, he'd be a happy man.

Noticing a crossing guard escorting children across the busy intersection, Clay got an idea.

Walking into the children's section of the Cliff Falls

Library, Clay approached the reference librarian. Here was the perfect compromise. *Everyone respected children's literature. All I have to do is quote a few books and write something akin to a graduation speech with a faith message tacked on the end. After all, most of what High Hope was used to was inspirational anyhow. Yep, Ted would be better served if I can just make him more likeable. If I do that, I will have accomplished a great task.*

Parents quietly read to their children as the librarian helped Clay gather the titles he requested. Most of the books, he was embarrassed to admit, he hadn't read until he was well into his twenties. He reasoned that while some adults revisited their childhood in their twenties and thirties, others were just trying to discover it.

Cramming his adult body into the miniature plastic chair, he sat at a children's table. The stack of classics covered the tabletop: *Charlotte's Web*, *The Giving Tree*, *The Outsiders*, and his personal favorite, *The Little Prince*. He transferred a memorable quote onto the back of a library index card with a crayon.

*"All grown-ups were children first. (But few remember it)."*

He marinated in the truth of the statement, although he personally knew a few adults he had suspected were never children. But that was beside the point. He had enough content in these books to compose something that at least showed he tried. No one could ask more than that.

"Tell me you're not going to use *The Little Prince*! Everyone quotes *The Little Prince*!"

Looking up, Clay discovered the blond mop top standing beside him.

"You're going to have to come up with something better than that if you're going to help my dad."

"How? What?"

"I was in the back of the balcony when you were talking to my grandfather," Tyler confessed.

Clay raised his eyebrows.

Tyler sorted through the other books. "*Oh, the Places You'll Go!* You got to be kidding? Original! We need something original here! Do I need to make a list?"

"Maybe you should help him?" Clay shot back.

"Shhhhh." The librarian placed her finger over her lips. They quieted down.

Clay recognized the silent anxiety in Tyler's eyes, a burden too heavy for any kid his age. He put down his crayon. "Why are you worried about all this, really?"

Tyler hesitated but knew he could trust him. "If my dad does a good job, my mom might transfer back here to Stanford."

"Did she tell you that?"

"I just think—"

"Tyler, it doesn't work that way. This is adult stuff. Your parents have to work it out for themselves."

But Tyler didn't want to hear it. He was convinced that he could fix anything with a little help. "Just promise me that you'll make my dad look good."

Tyler held out his pinkie finger. "Promise!"

Clay stared at the boy with bewilderment, finally giving in. "Pinkie swear."

# *Chapter Twenty-Four*

The typist entered "Clay Grant" into the Google search engine. 750,000 results appeared including:

"Mysterious Backlot Fire"
"LGM Sightings"
"Little Guy—Big Tax Debt"
"LGM: Dead or Alive—Urban Legends"
"CLAYHEART Auctions—*Little Guy Mike* Memorabilia"

*Click.* The eBay page opened revealing dozens of *Little Guy Mike* items up for auction as the page scrolled down. Bidding wars were in progress. Lots were cast for many of the same consumer products once destroyed by Clay, each listing with a colorful snapshot, current bid, and time remaining.

| "LGM Lunch Box and Thermos" | $149 | | 17h | 43m |
| "Autographed 8 by 10 headshot of Clay" | $77 | 1d | 12h | 19m |
| "'Little Guy Mike' Halloween mask" | $219 | 2d | 14h | 32m |
| "TV Guide featuring Clay on the cover" | $135 | 3d | 8h | 11m |

*Click.* The "Little Guy Mike" Halloween mask appeared on screen. It was a rare item and was in decent condition.

Ted stared at the happy plastic face with rosy cheeks, tempted to bid on the lot. He couldn't believe how popular the guy still was and what people were willing to pay for a piece of him. Whoever was running this site was making bank.

Ted glanced out his office window. What was his father thinking bringing this trouble here?

✳

Clay woke up early the next morning. He cracked the door open and felt the gentle breeze. Curling up in the blanket, he felt safe enough to sleep. It was amazing; he never realized how exhausted he was until he stopped running. But by afternoon he still hadn't written a word. As he sat on the woven oval rug on the floor of his loft apartment, he was already regretting the promise he made to Tyler. He knew the power of a pinkie swear was a binding contract. He didn't want to lie but he also didn't want to crush the boy's hope.

Clay reached into his pocket and looked over the list of instructions Tyler gave him, including what movie references not to use.

"No *Braveheart*, no *Matrix*, and especially no *Chariots of Fire*!"

Somehow the bar had just been raised. He couldn't care less about Ted, but that kid was another story. He had already let Bella down. He couldn't do the same to Tyler.

"I had forgotten how peaceful this loft was."

Clay looked up and saw Reagan standing in the doorway.

"As a young pastor, I wrote all my sermons here. I used to lock myself up here for days, writing at that desk, gazing out that window. This was the one place I could always escape to, even if just for a little while."

Clay started to get up, but Reagan motioned him not to bother. "I can't stay long."

"I don't want to screw this up for you." Holding Tyler's list in his hand, Clay understood more was at stake than even Reagan realized. "There's a lot riding on this. Get someone else. I'm sure you know people."

Reagan didn't want to hear it. "If you're having trouble writing, just dig deeper. I know what is inside of you."

Obviously, this man's grief had affected his judgment. But Clay realized that trying to convince him otherwise was no use.

"Why did you stop writing, Clay?"

Clay ran his fingers through his hair. "Words only made me more aware of what I could never change."

"That's a heavy burden." Reagan gripped the back of the chair. "What do you do with all that?"

"How do I cope? By staying one step ahead of it. I'm one of the lucky ones. Look at other child stars. I'm not a crackhead. I'm not dead."

Reagan nodded. "I don't know if it was a conscious decision, but the more popular I became, the less I put myself into my sermons. It happened so slowly that I don't think people noticed. Well, besides Rose. She'd always say, 'That's not the man I married.'

"I'd just tell the strongest stories over and over: the ones that portrayed me as a victor, overcoming an obstacle, but I'd never share the battles I was still fighting, the present self-doubt, the present pain. People needed a confident Reagan, and that is what I gave them."

"And I gave my audience what they wanted, happy, upbeat Clay. They weren't interested in the real me. No one was. I guess we have that in common. We get to keep those pieces of ourselves to ourselves."

Reagan turned to leave, glancing at the loft. "Rose was right. I never should have stopped writing here."

"She found me one night."

Reagan turned back.

"Crying after a fight with Burt on the tour. He beat the shit out of me. No one else knew what was going on, or if they did, they never let on, but she knew. I was embarrassed that she found me like that, but in that moment I knew I could trust her. I convinced her not to call the police because of the publicity, and I was angry when she called my mom, but knew she did it because she cared about me.

"When my mom called that night I thought she finally developed a spine, but then Burt twisted everything around, some explanation about me needing discipline and a strong male role model. She backed down. Ted was lucky to have a real mom."

"That man should have been locked up long ago." Reagan took a deep breath. "Was that the extent of the abuse?"

"Don't go there."

"You have to talk about this if you want to be healed. I want that for you."

"What do you want to hear? That he'd take pictures of me before I was old enough to fight back? That he'd manipulate me, whisper in my ear that if I told anyone that the photos would become public, the show would be canceled, and that my mom would be thrown out on the street? That we'd be banished outside the studio gate? I could tell you many sad stories but it would change nothing." Clay caught his breath. "Do you know the last time I spoke to my mother?"

"Was it that night?"

"The whole backlot was on fire. I took off on foot. My lungs were full of smoke, but I just ran as fast as I could. I didn't have anywhere to go. I was so scared. I could see helicopters overhead. I could hear sirens. I got about five miles away when I stopped and found a payphone. I had no other choice. Hyperventilating, I called her collect. 'Something terrible has happened.' But she already knew. I just kept saying, 'I want to come home. Please, I want to come home.' I was only eighteen. All I wanted to do was go home. She told me to go back.

"'Go back, Clay. It doesn't have to be over. *Burt* will handle it. Go back, son. *Burt* will take care of you.' That was the last time."

"Clay, everything that happened to you—"

Clay put his hand up to silence Reagan.

"I was twelve when I first realized that all the people-pleasing in the world would never make them love me or make my mom come back. It felt like a family, and everyone said it was, but it wasn't one, not really."

"You mattered to Rose. And you matter to me."

"That leather journal she gave me. I was nearly burned alive trying to save it." Clay got up and retrieved it from under the mattress, the rope still tied around it. "It's filled with every sad detail you'd ever want to know. I should have thrown it away years ago. A few times I almost did."

Reagan started to put his hand on Clay's shoulder but drew it back. "Maybe you kept it because even as a kid you knew everything that happened to you, mattered."

"Just because I didn't throw the journal away doesn't mean I need to relive all that junk. I don't need to remember what my life was really like. What it's like to be loved by a crowd who doesn't really know you. Bullied or abandoned by those who do know you. What it's like to be adored and resented all at the same time. No thank you." Clay caught his breath. "If that's what you expect from me to write this thing, you need to find someone else."

"Clay, I am so sorry no one protected you. You were only a boy."

Clay looked at Reagan and saw his eyes were full of tears. "I'm not that kid anymore."

"I'm not sure the kid inside of us ever goes away," Reagan said. "We just learn to neglect him. We stop listening to what he has to say. Maybe that kid is trying to tell you something?"

Clay clenched the journal in his hand.

Reagan knew Clay deserved to know what he had done. Omitting a truth was as bad as lying. "I'm embarrassed to admit this, but when I retrieved your journal, a page fell out and I read it. Forgive me. I didn't feel right reading more, but what I did read, it struck me to the core."

Clay looked at him stunned. "I haven't even read it. Not in years."

"That boy is still suffering. He is still in pain. I can't get his voice out of my mind."

"You don't know what you're asking. Do you know what

happened the last time I listened to that boy's voice?" Clay said, tightening his fingers around the journal. "The backlot burned."

"I am here for you. If you want to talk to someone professional I'll make that happen."

Clay held up his hand. It was all too much right now.

Reagan wanted to stay and be there for Clay, but sensed he wanted to be alone. It was against his instinct, but Reagan chose not to push the subject. He hoped he would have another chance once Clay had time to absorb what these memories evoked in him.

"All right," Reagan said. "But suffering can't stay hidden forever. The light will always find a way to reach it. When it does, don't be afraid to let it in."

As Reagan left, Clay tossed the journal onto the bed. Right now the knowledge that Reagan had read his journal paled in comparison to what these memories stirred up. Getting up, Clay went to the window. Looking out, he was once more mesmerized by the brook outside. He thought about searching for the elusive falls, but figured he was lost enough as it was. What he really needed to do was clear his head.

\*

Wandering down by the babbling brook at the base of the hillside, Clay felt drained. All he wanted was to be a thousand miles away from civilization and from anyone who could hurt him. Putting his hand in the trickling water, he'd like to believe that the stream really did originate from the falls everyone talked about.

Why do I always feel like the weight of everyone else's life is always on my shoulders?

*Beads of sweat dripped down his forehead, melting the pancake makeup on his face. Throat dry, he couldn't speak. He could feel them all around him, staring from the rafters, from the wings and from behind the camera, waiting, and every eye on him. All their jobs rested on how he delivered his lines.*

*The show was struggling to find its audience. Network was thinking of pulling the plug. One executive said a game show would do better at 8:00 pm on a Tuesday night and would be cheaper to produce.*

*The week before, his friend's series got canceled after five years. The poor kid learned about it by reading it in the trades. Now the guy wasn't even allowed on the lot. When the kid and his mom came back the next afternoon to clean out his dressing room they were turned away at the security gate by the same guy who greeted them every day for the past five years.*

*Clay delivered the catch phrase and all he heard was laughter. Everyone in the wings and everyone on the rafters was smiling. He knew he would have to make that happen every time.*

He had come out here to clear his head. Why did all these memories keep coming back to him? He shook the water from his hands, stood up, and moved on.

Clay traced the brook upstream hoping his memories would dissipate in the sound of babbling water. No such luck.

He followed the weathered fence towards the north side of the property, spotting a High Hope truck outside the old barn. It was about as beaten up as the barn itself.

The old barn was a shell of a structure. If not for it being the oldest building on the campus, it would have been knocked down years ago.

Clay pulled the door back, the hinges creaking from the effort. He stepped into the barn and was awestruck by what he discovered.

The golden beams poured in from the rafters through cracks in the shingled roof, illuminating the canvases that littered the barn.

The paintings hung on rusty hooks nailed to the timber, their violent purple and red strokes contrasting with the decaying wood that surrounded them. Each captured a moment on a sorrowful path, the progression of a contorted body and injured flesh. There must have been a dozen.

Clay hesitated, feet planted in the dirt below, as the weary eyes cried out to him. He recognized the sequence. It was *The Way of the Cross*, a series of paintings depicting the final hours of Jesus' life.

The anguish of a twisted torso bloodied by the lashes of rage. The laughing faces of ridicule. A shoulder slumping under the pressure of the splintered beam, knees collapsing under the weight, falling to the ground. Fingers pointed in judgment. Lots cast for clothing. The mockery of a purple cloak.

The paintings evoked something more inside of him than other inspirational art he had seen. Perhaps it was the sum of the collection, that each moment had been memorialized, that each moment mattered. Or maybe it was that they were hidden within this weathered barn. All he knew was that he felt like he was stepping onto sacred ground.

He moved forward as dust particles danced in the light, the hallowed paintings on either side of him drawing him in. It seemed as if he were taking part in the journey, a bystander in the crowd looking on.

With each step he was increasingly aware of the determined eyes as the rays continued to seep in through the splintered wood. For a moment he couldn't tell if the light was pouring in or pouring out.

An easel stood in the middle of the barn. It was a work-in-progress, the artist's jagged pencil sketch hidden by the seemingly random strokes of the brush.

Clay moved in closer. He could see the dripping paint, the colors bleeding, bubbling, and attempting to dry from the light that bled through the fractured wood. He had seen other versions a thousand times before, but only now did he understand it: It was Hope taking its last breath.

He would have stared at the canvas forever if he had not been interrupted.

"It's far from complete." Diego stood a few feet away carrying a pail filled with turpentine and several brushes.

"You did all this?"

"Not all at once."

"They are amazing. Really, I wouldn't just say that. You should show them. Have an art show. Hang them in the sanctuary or something." Clay couldn't get over the vividness of the paintings or what they stirred in him.

"It just feels good to get paint on your hands." For Diego, creating for an audience of One was enough. Everything didn't need to be exploited or marketed or end up on a calendar or a PowerPoint slide during worship.

"I'm telling you, these are beautiful," Clay said.

"Have you ever considered what God created that will never be seen by human eyes, like fish in the depths of the sea? What He created just because that's what a Creator does? I think about that all the time."

"Unfortunately, most of what I've created I wouldn't consider art."

"It's like a kid's painting. If your heart is in it, it's art."

Clay felt conviction stir up inside of him even though his heart wasn't part of the deal. He glanced at the paintings again and then back at Diego. "You know that old truck out front. Does it still run?"

"I think we can get her going."

Diego handed Clay keys to the weathered High Hope truck.

Climbing in, Clay felt the springs and coils in the seat. Turning the key, he started the engine. It sputtered, exhaust pouring out of the tailpipe.

"I'm assuming this didn't pass a smog check," Clay said over the engine's rumble.

"We plant a tree every time we take her out." Diego smiled.

Offering directions, Diego pointed down the dirt road. The truck pulled away.

*

The flashing neon sign out front read "The Dutch Goose". He was about eight miles from Hope, but it felt like the edge of civilization. Inside, the dimly lit room was crowded with a mix of Stanford students and technology professionals unwinding after work. The pool tables and peanuts seemed to be the main attractions.

Clay sat at the bar with a blank notepad, watching SportsCenter, cracking and eating peanuts. Something about the barn had inspired him.

The pile of shells surrounding his portion of the counter grew as thoughts were written down and then promptly crossed out. It had been a while since he put his heart into anything.

"Can I get you another?" the bartender asked.

Clay looked up from writing. "How does this sound?" He read from the pad.

> "It's one thing to believe in something when you don't need it to be true. It's another when everything is riding on it."

"Sounds like you've been eating too much Chinese food."

Clay crossed out the line figuring he'd have been better off with a bag of fortune cookies for inspiration.

"But don't take my word for it," the portly bartender backtracked. "I'm not very deep. At least that's what Tommy says. We should ask Tommy. Tommy's smart. Tommy has his doctorate in philosophy. Hey, Tommy, how does this sound?"

Tommy sat at the opposite end of the bar. He had a narrow beard and wore a T-shirt with a portrait of Rasputin. He responded with a reluctant, but curious gaze.

This was not exactly Clay's target audience but he had nothing to lose. Reluctantly, he repeated the line. "It's one thing to believe in something when you don't need it to be true. It's another when everything is riding on it."

Clay and the bartender waited in silence as Tommy stared at them as if he had just tasted a foreign Merlot with unfamiliar characteristics. He seemed unwilling to either smile or spit it out. Clay would have preferred either reaction.

"Interesting," Tommy said in a detached, analytical tone. "And by 'believe' you mean what exactly?"

Clay tried to explain. "How do you know what you *really* believe unless you have had to rely on it? Unless something was at stake?"

"Interesting," he said again in the same non-committal tone, somehow incapable of emoting. "And by 'rely,' you mean what exactly?"

All Clay could think was if Tommy went to Stanford, he should get his money back. "That's all right, really. If I have to explain it, it's probably not working."

Crumpling up the paper, Clay turned his attention to the peanuts and SportsCenter.

After a few moments an attractive woman smiled at him. Not his type; he was more interested in the peanuts. Finally, she gave up.

As she walked away, the unthinkable happened. A TVLand commercial announcing a *Little Guy Mike* weekend marathon was broadcast on the televisions throughout the bar.

"*Looking for* 'Little Guy Mike'*? Well, we know where you can find him. Right here on TVLand!*"

Clay could not believe what he was seeing. His childhood face lit up the place.

"*It's a* Little Guy Mike *Weekend! 48 hours of back-to-back episodes!*"

The portly bartender got excited. "I love that show!"

Clay sunk into his bar stool trying to disappear.

College students began singing *One Dream Short: The Ballad of Little Guy Mike*. Soon the whole bar joined in. Even Tommy knew the words!

*"One dream short from touching the sky.*
*Then along came one lit-tle guy.*
*Now the impossible is just around the bend.*
*Thanks to our new lit-tle friend.*
*He's our guy—aye, aye, aye—lit-tle guy.*
*He's our guy—aye, aye, aye—lit-tle guy. Little Guy Mike!*

Clay pulled down his knit hat, got up, and quietly slipped out of the bar.

*

The street was crowded as he drove down University Avenue in Palo Alto. It was backed up from the weekly farmer's market. He moved slowly through the heavy traffic, the windows rolled down and the cold breeze blowing in his face.

Blasting the radio, he tried to get that damn theme song out of his head. It was insidious, designed to overtake any other thought. If anything made him want to run, it was *that* song. He spotted the Caltrain station in the distance.

The farmer's market was in full swing, bustling with

families, seniors and the young professionals who lived and worked in the area. This had also become a weekly ritual for Becky, who took the train in after work and always headed to the flower vendor first. No matter what kind of day she was having, the sight of flowers was usually enough to lift her spirits. Besides, she liked carrying the flowers with her as she made her way through the rest of the market. This evening was no different.

It wasn't hard to spot the sunflowers beyond the Gerber daisies and peonies. She sorted through the buckets, her auburn hair tied in a scarf, and waitress uniform peeking out from the oversized sweater she was wearing.

Finally, she held up two bunches of sunflowers, one in each hand. She shook off the excess water and took a moment to compare the two.

"The bunch on your left."

Becky was surprised to discover Clay standing beside her; his confident eyes and defined jaw framed by the knit hat he was wearing.

"Clearly. They're brighter, more confident. Overall, a happier bunch." Clay offered a self-assured smile.

"And these?" She held up the bunch in her right hand.

"They look *less* happy, kind of sad and insecure. They have fewer petals and leaves. Overall, I don't think they can give you what you need."

Becky studied both again and then, aware of her own need, made a confident choice: the *less* happy bunch in her right hand. "These," she told the vendor.

Clay was taken aback.

"They're lonely. They need me."

Clay had a sense that he had met his match. As the vendor tore a piece of brown butcher paper to wrap up the flowers, Clay subtly changed gears. "So I guess all I need to know is your address."

"I've had plenty of guys ask for my phone number, but my address?" Becky paid the vendor. "A little aggressive, don't you think?"

"Oh, I'm not asking you out. Did you think I was asking you out? I just need your address so I can deliver your 'lonely' flowers."

"Painful. You are so painful."

"Me? I looked like an idiot showing up with that coffee cake."

"I feel terrible." Becky bit her lip to contain her laughter.

"I'm sure you do."

Becky regained her composure. "So how's it going, at the church?"

"I'm in over my head. I think it's time to start planning my exit."

"That's too bad."

The vendor handed Becky the sunflowers.

"Look, while I am here, I really would like to see you again."

"I'm done dating guys who are just passing through. I've been there, done that."

"Don't think of it as passing through. Think of it as, drive-thru dating."

Becky gave him a stare before he could backtrack.

"Okay, maybe that's not a good analogy."

Becky shook her head. Somehow his goofiness was part of his charm.

"Come on."

But Becky wouldn't budge.

"All right. All right. No dating," Clay made the official declaration. "There will be no dating!" After a moment, he tried another angle. "How about walking? Can I walk with you? No dating. Just walking?"

Becky was suspect, but somehow he had worn her down. "I guess that would be all right."

They made their way into the farmer's market.

"You know it's tough times for churches."

"Really?"

"When I delivered the coffee cake, they didn't even tip."

Becky smiled.

"By the way, that California Tiramisu at the Acorn. It was terrible."

"It tastes fine to me."

"That's the problem. You never know you've got the fake thing, unless you've had the real thing."

"For me, it's not that simple," Becky countered. "Sometimes the question isn't if something is real or fake. Sometimes the question is, 'How real is it?'"

"Well, the real thing will silence all those doubts," Clay grinned. "Hey, if we ever do go out on a real date, I'll teach you how to make real Tiramisu."

"You bake?"

"I'm full of hidden talents."

&#42;

A woman forged Clay's signature onto a box containing

a "Little Guy Mike" action figure. She placed a "Certified Authenticated Signature" sticker on the back and then packed it in a carton for shipping.

She had told herself that she was going to go to bed early tonight but she knew she still had a few hours of work ahead of her. Things always picked up whenever Clay was in the news. Although it had been years, any news was good news because at least it was news.

She gathered the rest of the packages for the post office that she would drop off in the morning. Settling at her computer, she uploaded snapshots of the new merchandise onto her website, CLAYHEART Auctions. The site had a reputation for selling both merchandise and rare personal items that once belonged to Clay.

The doorbell rang.

Getting up to answer the door, she passed family photos on the wall. The faded pictures were of a shy boy and his mother.

Patty Grant opened the door and was surprised to discover Burt standing before her. She tried to shut the door, but was blocked by Burt's foot in the doorjamb.

"I don't know where he is, and if I did, I wouldn't tell you," she snapped.

Burt glanced at all the packages in the entry. He cocked his head. "Some people would call you a terrible mom for how you make your living, forging his signature. Selling all this *Little Guy Mike* junk on eBay," he said sarcastically. "But not me. What else were you supposed to do when that kid took off and stopped supporting you?"

He inched his foot further in the door, feeling her ease

her grasp.

"Leave him alone."

"He owes me! He owes all of us!"

"I never should have trusted you," she whispered.

Burt pushed his way into the entry and pulled out his wallet.

"I don't need your money," Patty said without looking at him.

"He doesn't care about you! He doesn't care about anyone but himself!"

"That's not true."

"When are you going to wake up? He made a fool out of all of us."

"It wasn't his fault."

"Nothing is ever his fault! He's just a poor little victim, right?"

"You're all going to burn in hell for what you've done to him," Patty said.

Burt got in her face. "And you along with us!"

He snapped his wallet shut and stuffed it in his jeans. "I will find him, with or without your help!" Burt took a good look at all the packages by the door before turning and walking way. "And when I do..."

Patty paused, and then called out to Burt with desperation in her voice, "Hey." Burt turned to look at her, anticipating a clue. "If you do find him..." She hesitated knowing that whatever she said could never make up for what she had done. Her voice faltered. "Never mind."

Patty watched as her only connection to her son turned and walked away. She closed the door.

✳

Clay and Becky walked through the farmer's market passing arts and crafts, food and produce vendors. Although they were not on a date, it looked a lot like one.

A small crowd gathered around a jazz quartet playing Bossa Nova. The quartet was pretty good.

An older Jewish man with a thick Yiddish accent began humming along to *The Girl From Ipanema*, his hands and head swaying to the unhurried rhythm. His spirit was contagious, transforming the highbrow mood into a joyful experience. He spotted Becky and tried to romance her away from Clay.

Clay and Becky shared a smile before moving on.

They stopped at a gourmet tamale stand and split the blue corn tamale with green chili.

"Did you meet Max?" Becky asked.

"The guy in the ridiculous golfing clothes who looks like Randy Quaid?"

"He's my brother."

"Did I mention Randy Quaid is a good-looking dude? Dennis Quaid has nothing on him. If you ask me, Meg Ryan went for the wrong Quaid."

"He's the only family I have. I moved here a few months ago after my dad passed."

"I'm sorry."

"I wasn't even living near my dad. I hadn't seen him in years. But once it happened..." Becky caught herself. "I don't even know why I'm telling you all this."

"No, I appreciate you sharing your heart. Really."

"Once it happened, I felt like being closer to family." Becky glanced at her lonely sunflowers again. "Don't say anything, but he's thinking of moving."

"Would you go with him?"

Becky shook her head, no. "For once, I'm going to stay put. He has his own family, and I like it here."

"I don't want you to think I'm a quitter," Clay said, "but I'm in a tough situation." Maybe it was because she had opened up first, or perhaps he needed her to understand, but either way he felt he could trust her. At least with this. Without telling Becky the specifics, Clay tried to explain his dilemma in the vaguest terms possible. "And this person doesn't want my help."

Becky looked right at him, "You're writing Ted's sermon?"

Clay's eyes widened, "I didn't say that!"

"Your secret is safe with me. My lips are sealed."

"Let's just say...had I known what they expected of me before I came, I probably never would have come."

"But you are here now."

"It's not that easy."

Becky listened as they moved toward the candle vendor. The tent was beautifully lit with the glimmering candles glowing against the night sky. They stopped and sniffed a few scents: pear, orange spice, and jasmine.

"This assignment...it's hard to find the words."

"Look, it's none of my business, but have you tried? Really tried?"

"What would it change?"

Becky stared at the flickering candles. "When my dad

was living, neither one of us could find the words. It's strange. Now that he's gone, they come so easily. I catch myself talking to him all the time. Only he's not there."

She glanced at Clay.

"It's important to find the words while they can still do some good."

\*

"My homework?" Tyler spoke into the receiver. "It's coming along just fine, Mom."

Ted raised his head out of the elementary school textbook and shot Tyler a perplexed look. He sat at the dining room table beside the folded laundry and empty frozen dinner containers. A moment ago the answers were clear; now he was second-guessing himself.

"You know Dad's preaching this Sunday, and they're announcing it!"

Ted erased the answers he had just written, blowing the particles away.

"I already told you that?" Tyler said. He held his hand over the phone and quietly pleaded with his dad. "Talk to her."

Ted looked up, staring at the receiver. Their last conversation hadn't gone well. Flight arrangements for the service quickly digressed into how she couldn't pretend everything was perfect anymore, that she didn't feel needed, that there was no place in his life for her, and how he always picked the church over her. He had told her that if she wasn't going to stay then she shouldn't come back for the funeral. He never thought she wouldn't be there.

Tyler held out the phone and waited. "Please?"

Ted reluctantly reached for the phone, but hesitated.

Tyler watched in disappointment as his dad abruptly got up from the table and left the room.

"Tyler, are you still there?" His mom's echo reverberated from the receiver.

"Yeah, Mom. I'm still here." The boy held the phone tighter. "I'm still here."

*

Clay walked Becky to the Caltrain station. "Are you sure I can't give you a ride home?"

"It's only a few stops," she replied, cradling her sunflowers.

"You don't know what you're passing up. Not everyone gets to ride in the High Hope truck."

Her hazel eyes lit up each time she smiled. It made him want to do whatever he could to see that happen again.

They came near the platform, passing a couple that gave them an "aren't you a romantic couple" smile.

"I know we're just walking and all, but people could get the wrong idea," Clay said.

"How so?" Becky didn't want to admit that she was feeling something stronger than she was letting on.

"Flowers..." he said quietly. He moved in closer.

She watched his eyes stare at her lonely bouquet.

"Moonlight..."

She followed his gaze upward, their eyes searching for the moon beneath the thick fog that was rolling in. They waited until they could spot its illuminated presence.

"An amazing woman." Lowering his gaze, he looked at her, waiting for that brightness to re-appear in her eyes. When he saw it, he eased in for the kiss.

Becky hesitated, trying to remember her rationale for keeping emotional distance. "I don't kiss on the first...."

Clay placed his index finger gently on her lips. "This isn't a date, remember."

Becky squeezed her bouquet as he leaned in.

He kissed her softly. The vulnerability of the moment lingered before the embarrassment settled in.

The Caltrain approached the station.

"I better get going."

He watched her move towards the train.

"By the way, you were right," Clay said.

Becky looked back, cradling her bouquet.

"The sunflowers. They look happier already." He saw the brightness in her eyes as she boarded the train. As the platform emptied, Clay watched the train leave the station.

✳

Heavy fog rolled in as Clay drove back to the church, the truck's headlights revealing only a few feet ahead of him as he traveled along the winding mountain road.

Parking the truck, he closed the old barn doors and walked across campus through the dense fog.

As he passed Rose's memorial garden that Diego had been busy working in, Clay thought he heard weeping.

Moving forward, he noticed that the wrought iron gate was open. Through the thick fog he made out a figure. It was

Ted. He was at his mother's grave, reading from a crumpled paper in his hand. It sounded like a eulogy.

"Everyone felt like she was their mother. But she was my mother." Ted took pride in the statement before continuing. "And she always saw, in all of us, what we could never see in ourselves. That was her gift."

Clay watched from a distance.

Ted looked lost as he stared at the memorial gravestone. Moving more closely, he got down on bended knee.

Putting down the paper, Ted spoke to her as if she were there. It was a whole different Ted.

"I'm sorry mom. I tried. I'll never be able to fill dad's shoes." He wept. "I'm always trying. But it doesn't matter. I can't make anything work." Ted sobbed. "I'm sorry. I'm just so sorry."

What had started out sounding like a eulogy had become a confession. Clay did not feel right listening in. He moved on in the dense cover of fog.

Clay returned to his loft apartment. Tossing the truck's keys onto the dresser, he took out his wallet and removed a scrap of paper. He sat on the side of the bed, staring at the phone number. Clay picked up the receiver to the rotary phone and began dialing. As the phone rang he felt a hesitation.

Two thousand miles away Patty Grant turned on a lamp beside her bed and answered the phone. "Hello."

Clay hesitated, the sound of his mother's voice transporting him back to his youth.

"Hello? Clay is that you?" Her voice was desperate, yet hopeful.

Clay hung up the phone.

# *Chapter Twenty-Five*

The Acorn was bustling with the usual morning rush, but he had arrived when they first unlocked the doors, before the set-ups were on the tables and the coffee cake had come out of the oven.

It was empty except for his thoughts.

He had settled into a booth, trying to separate himself not only from the patrons who would be trickling in, but from the sound of his mother's voice that had filled up his once-sacred loft.

Although it was a new day, it felt like a continuation from the night before. And the cellophane toothpicks overhead gave him no direction.

Like that old journal he refused to read, he knew better than to open any door to his past. So why did he decide to carry it in his backpack today?

He couldn't get beyond the image of Ted speaking to his mother through the thick fog. But Rose was a saint. She hadn't exploited her own son and then abandoned him right when he needed her the most, turning him over to handlers with their own financial motives. He caught himself. He knew where that rabbit-hole led and wanted to bring as little of that junk into this new day as possible.

Turning his attention to the task at hand, he removed a pad of paper from his backpack and tried to see what he could come up with.

As the diner filled up, his table became covered with crumpled paper. Obviously, he was not having much luck. He found it hard to write while keeping those feelings at bay, torn by the impossibility of opening up and shutting down at the same time. He knew he should be stronger, able to rise above it, but he just couldn't. And that is why he always tried to stay at least one step ahead of it.

Staring at a blank piece of paper, he got a thought and wrote it down.

*"I always wanted to be a man of steel."*

He stared at the page, trying to complete his thought, finally adding,

*"Unfortunately, I'm just Clay."*

Crumpling up the paper, he added it to the pile.

Clay looked around the diner for inspiration. No luck.

He glanced at the art-deco mural above the counter, the rustic faces of city workers and ranch hands crossing paths in front of the feed store in the 1930's, painted golden rays shining down on both. He was always looking for a glimpse of

Heaven, but had yet to find it.

Staring at their faces, Clay felt it was as if they were trying to tell him something, that the promise hidden in their eyes was realized as they crossed paths in front of the feed store and that he belonged among them.

He admired the mural and its message of brotherhood but thought about the paintings he had seen in the barn: the truth about the cruelty of man that was not exclusive to any race.

It occurred to him that he also could not write because he knew better than to be idealistic. He understood the danger of believing in an idea divorced from the reality he always knew. For him, that only led to disappointment. The hope could never be sustained. In the end, people always hurt you. He concluded that the message of that mural, however beautiful, was imposed by the idealism of the artist. He didn't want to do the same.

A waitress approached him with a pot of coffee.

He quickly put his hand over his mug.

"Why stop now?" The waitress grimaced before moving on.

"I was afraid you'd start charging me for refills."

Turning his attention, he gazed out the window and spotted Becky crossing the street. Happily distracted, he watched her.

He couldn't get over it. She was perfect: the hair, the hazel eyes, the legs, just the right combination of sweet and feisty that kept him on his toes. He didn't know if he was idealizing her or just really seeing who she was. He only knew that he was drawn to this quality in her that transcended everything else. It was hope dwelling in a place of sadness.

To him, that meant more than anything else he had heard or seen.

She made her way into the diner, saying hello to her co-workers. Moving behind the counter, she placed her apron over her uniform and secured it.

Clay picked up his empty coffee cup, walked to the counter and took a seat. "What does a guy have to do to get a refill around here?"

Becky was surprised to see him. "I was curious if you'd still be here."

"You didn't think I was going to skip town, not after last night?"

"I wasn't sure." She reached for the pot of coffee and filled his mug up. "I'm still not sure."

"This relationship is never going to work unless you have a little faith in me," he said half-jokingly.

Becky rolled her eyes. She thought he looked a little disheveled, like he hadn't slept, but somehow the look worked on him.

"I've been here all morning. I'm trying. I really am."

"Any luck?" She noticed the crumpled papers on his table.

Leaning over the counter, Clay whispered into her ear. "The words are in hiding. They don't want to be found. I don't blame them."

She looked at him with assurance. "Don't worry. You'll find them."

He perked up. "So you do have faith in me?"

Becky laughed.

"Maybe you're trying too hard? There are great hiking trails just up the hillside."

"And go in search of the majestic falls?"

"Are you afraid you're going to get lost?"

"I'm afraid of finding them and being disappointed. I'm afraid of them not living up to the hype."

"You can do this." Becky gave him an encouraging smile.

"I'm thinking that the real problem isn't that I can't write it; it's that I have a problem getting people's hopes up." He glanced at the rustic faces in the mural again. "I want to be honest. I want to be true to my life experience. Unfortunately, that's not very inspirational." He caught himself. He couldn't believe he just admitted to a beautiful woman that he didn't think his life was very inspirational.

"But you said they want to hear your perspective?"

"Yeah, but this is going to be public, so I don't want to cause problems."

"Maybe you don't need to worry about being inspirational. Maybe being honest is enough."

"The church is called 'High Hope', not 'slightly disappointed'."

The first waitress passed by and noticed Clay drinking another cup of coffee. She shook her head before moving on.

"I've had a few cups already," he admitted to Becky. It was an understated confession that fooled no one.

"I figured that," Becky said.

"I'm giving this my best shot." Clay rolled up his sleeves. "Look, I'm literally rolling up my sleeves."

Becky noticed a scar on his arm just below his elbow. "How did you get that? It must have hurt."

"Oh, that's from when I crashed into you with the coffee cake."

"What?"

"I'm just kidding. I took a tumble down a flight of stairs when I was a kid. Clumsy. It was nothing." He changed the subject. "Look, I have to work on this assignment right now, but I thought maybe later tonight we could hang out again? Find another farmer's market or something."

"I can't."

"You have plans?"

"It's not that. I told you last night. I can't pursue this any further if you're not going to be sticking around. I've lost a lot of people in my life. Honestly, I can't take it."

"Hey, this is a risk for me too. How do I know that once you really get to know me you won't dump me for the next lovable, slightly disappointed, scruffy-faced hunk that comes to town?"

"I guess the only way you'll know for sure is if you stick around."

He rolled his eyes. "I don't like it, but I'll respect it. I won't try to change your mind. I promise." Clay grinned.

✳

Alexis, Max, Thomas, Maggie, Paul and Monica exited after the day's staff meeting, pausing in the corridor as Reagan, Ted and the rest of the staff continued on. They shared glances, somehow surprised that Reagan had not come to his senses.

"Maybe Reagan's setting Ted up?" Thomas was always the conspiracy theorist.

Alexis shook her head no.

"Think about it. Get him up to bat quick. Strike him out fast. It makes sense."

"At least it makes some sense," Max said.

Busy with her Palm Pilot, Maggie was insistent. "No father is going to sacrifice his son, even if it is for the sake of the church."

"No father is going to sacrifice his son?" Max shot Maggie a look. "We really need to rent you *The Passion of the Christ*."

Maggie was confused as the group laughed.

Paul spoke up, "You'd think Reagan would grow tired of being the king of 'outside the box'? It's exhausting."

Thomas replied, "Reagan is so 'outside the box' that at this point the most 'outside the box' idea he could have would be an idea that was actually 'in the box'!"

"That's what I always loved about him," Max said.

"Loved?" Thomas replied.

"So, Max," Monica pressed the subject, "word has it that Pearl Street Pond has come a-calling."

Max looked at Alexis.

"I swear it wasn't me," Alexis said. "Well, I didn't tell Monica, but I may have mentioned it to Reagan."

"Confidentiality, Alexis! You're a licensed therapist," Max said.

"So you are leaving?" Monica said.

"That's not something I want made public right now. Especially in light of everything that's going on here."

"Hey, we all did our best," Paul said. "If this place implodes, my hands are clean."

"Hands clean?" Alexis said. "I just watched you eat two hunks of coffee cake without a fork."

Paul took stock of his buttery hands. "Well, you get my point."

"You know that guy who delivered the coffee cake the other day?" Thomas said. "I think he's staying on property, in the loft."

"Maybe Reagan's hiring replacements already?" Paul said.

"At least someone is coming and not going," Alexis responded.

"Yeah, but for how long?" Monica replied.

✳

Outside the Acorn, Clay held the wooden ladder steady, staring at Becky's shapely legs. He knew he should be writing but this was a welcome distraction.

As Becky hammered above, Clay hummed *The Girl From Ipanema*, doing his best impression of the Yiddish man from the night before.

"*Ya, da, da, da, ya, da, da, ya, ya...*"

"Stop humming that!"

"Not until you go out with me," Clay's request interspersed with more humming.

"That guy was charming. You're like one of those annoying boys I used to beat up on the playground." Becky held out her hand.

"I'm trying." Clay handed her the flagpole. "That has to count for something."

"I just don't want to get hurt again."

"Well, what am I supposed to do until I do know if I'm staying put?" He helped her down the ladder.

Becky thought for a moment, conjuring up a suitable compromise. "You can always visit me at the counter."

"The counter?" Clay balked with lovable outrage.

"The counter is a great place to hang out."

Stepping off the ladder, Becky took a look at the patchwork flag she had made. It read "Welcome".

Clay glanced at the flag and then back at Becky, feeling anything but welcome. "What is so *special* about the counter?"

"Do you know what I see when I work the counter?"

"People chewing?"

Becky moved towards the plate glass window. Clay followed. They observed the counter. It was full. They could see people's backs and side profiles.

"Most times I see an amazing mix of people," Becky said. "Every kind of person you can imagine, all lined up, and seated side by side. People who would never interact outside of this place, taking time to come together, share a bit of their lives. A bit of their lives with some stranger on the left or right of them." She pressed her hand on the glass. "To me, that's holy."

"I don't think I'm ever going to look at a diner the same way again."

"They say once, in the early years, it rained so hard that the road leading up to the church washed out. These days, people would see that as a sign to stay home. But back then, meeting together was central to life around here. So that Sunday, they held church right here at the Acorn. People just gathered around the counter, muddy mess and all.

"Don't get me wrong, this job can be a drag. But there are those moments. Those little glimpses of Heaven."

"That's beautiful. Can I steal it?"

Becky held up the hammer. "Those are my words. You have to find your own."

"The problem with my words is that they sound too much like me. I can't do this. I was sitting at the counter, and I didn't see any of that *humanity*. I was annoyed at how close everyone was to me." Clay was worked up. "I can't use Ted's words, and I can't find my own. This is going to get ugly. It always does. 'Nothing gold can stay.' That's from *The Outsiders*."

"I think it was Robert Frost."

"Him too?" Clay asked. He looked at the counter again. "I'm so tired of feeling guilty."

"Too bad you're not Catholic, you could go to confession."

"This is not my fault this time—"

"They say it cleans out the pipes. St. Anthony's is just down the road."

"I don't need confession. Words, I need words."

Becky was self-reflective. "But how do you find the words if you've never heard them?"

"All I know is that the wrong words stay with you a lot longer than the right ones." Clay felt a familiar desperation. "I don't want to disappoint Tyler. I don't want to disappoint Reagan. I don't want to disappoint you, but what does everyone expect of me?"

"Well, I guess that's my answer." Becky walked back into the Acorn.

"Don't give up on me yet!" Clay turned around and saw Tyler standing beside him. He was in his school uniform, tightening the straps on his *Dinosaur Kingdom* backpack.

"You're supposed to be writing!" Tyler said. "Not talking to girls!"

"And you're supposed to be in school," Clay shot back.

"It's a minimum day." Tyler tugged Clay by the shirt.

"Come with me! There's something I need to show you!"

Grabbing his own backpack, Clay followed Tyler along the rolling hillside, the light wind ruffling his hair. They traced the flowing brook upward. In the distance, Clay saw the silhouette of a well-built tree house atop a towering tree trunk. Out of breath, they reached the base of the tree. Hand over hand, they climbed the ladder like Clay had climbed the scaffolding as a boy. Opening the hatch, Tyler and Clay hoisted themselves up, removing their backpacks and tossing them in the corner. Clay looked out the window at gentle green hills, with homes pocketing the landscape. He could see for miles.

"It's like we're on top of the world up here."

"I told you. This is the perfect place to write." Tyler handed him markers and paper. "Everything you need, right here."

"You have thought of everything." Clay picked up a deck of cards. "Go Fish?"

"Five-card draw!" Tyler said. "Three hands and then you write!"

"Poker it is." Clay shuffled the cards and dealt.

"Can I ask you a question?" Tyler asked.

"Sure."

"Were you closer to your mom or dad?" Tyler picked up the cards and gave them a quick look.

"I didn't have a dad," Clay said, looking at his cards disgusted.

"You didn't have a dad?"

"Nope. When I was young I was really close to my mom. But even that changed."

"You stopped loving your mom?"

"It wasn't like that. I worked as a kid."

"You had a job, like my dad?"

"Something like that," Clay said. He drew another card. No luck. "I was sent away and at first she came with me, but then that changed. You're lucky. You have a mom and a dad who love you. Not to mention a grandfather."

"He built this tree house," Tyler said proudly.

"See what I mean."

"So you never had a family?"

"Well, the people I worked with were sort of a family. We certainly looked like one. But I missed my mom." Clay put his cards down. "You miss your mom, right?"

"Oh, yeah." Tyler looked like he could cry. It was a familiar look Clay understood all too well.

"When I was young I had a place just like this."

"You had a tree house?" Tyler said with excitement.

"Not exactly. There were all these metal structures where I worked. Scaffolding. They were about as high as this." Clay leaned in. "At night, when I missed my mom, I'd climb the scaffolding and settle into my usual spot." Clay looked out the tree house window. "I swear, Tyler, you could touch the stars. It was the one place I could find peace. The one place I could exhale."

"What would you do up there?" Tyler asked.

"I'd write. Until the early morning hours."

"That's what you need to do now!" Tyler handed him the paper and markers.

"That was a long time ago."

"You promised you'd try!"

"I am, Tyler. But this isn't your fight."

"You don't believe that! You're like me. You would have done anything to bring your mom back, right?"

A voice yelled in the distance, "TYLER!!"

Clay and Tyler clenched their cards.

"I thought you said it was a minimum day?" Clay asked.

Tyler shrugged his shoulders. "I took the rest of the day off."

Clay reached for his backpack but Tyler stopped him.

"You stay up here and write!" Tyler opened the hatch and scrambled down the ladder. "You have to help my dad. Time is running out!"

If Clay was anything it was resilient. He would find another way. If he couldn't steal the words, he now had an idea where he could borrow them.

*

Ted proudly held his sermon in hand as he walked down the corridor towards his father's office. He had optimism in his step.

He passed Monica.

"Looking forward to Sunday, Ted!" Monica said offering an enthusiastic thumbs-up as she passed.

"Why, thank you, Monica." Ted was flattered. The announcement had gone out, so the town knew he would be preaching by now. Maybe he had more support than he had imagined?

Reagan was on the phone when Ted knocked on his open door. He had spent the day putting out fires and the largest one had yet to ignite.

"You wanted to see me?" Ted asked.

Reagan stared at his son with a pensive look. "Have a seat."

"I almost have my talk committed to memory, but of course I want it loaded in the teleprompter just in case."

"About that message. I think we should save it for another day."

"Another day?" Ted was devastated. He knew he should have seen this coming. With his father there was always a catch. "Let me guess, I'm not preaching anymore."

"Indeed, you are. Just not *that*, " Reagan pointed to his sermon. "I want to set you up to win. 'Juanita Gonzalez' is the old Ted. Not the 'new-improved Ted' that we want to introduce to everyone."

"What am I, laundry detergent?"

"We're going in a new direction," Reagan said. "I expect you to trust me on this."

Wadding up the sermon in his hand, Ted knew it would be scrapped just like the eulogy he had composed for his mother. "So I assume you're writing my sermon. Again."

"Not exactly."

Ted's eyes widened. "But if I'm not writing it and you're not, who is?"

Reagan smiled warmly.

&ast;

The sign out front announced the mid-day mass. Clay crossed the street and made his way into the modest Catholic Church in downtown Cliff Falls.

Mass was in progress. The sparse parish stood reciting a

prayer. These were the faithful. They were at church in the middle of the day and it wasn't even a holiday. He moved down the side aisle as light poured in through the stained glass windows.

Trying to be discreet, Clay slipped into a pew beside an elderly woman with very clear diction. He tried to follow along but the prayer was slightly different from the one he was familiar with. The elderly woman gave him an encouraging smile as he stumbled through it.

For all his criticism of High Hope, it did occur to him that this place could use a television or two so visitors could follow the prayer. And while they were at it, state-of-the-art lighting and a new sound system. He didn't want to be a critic. It was just that they obviously had the "holy" down and he thought they could benefit from some better production values, and maybe a digital screen and retractable stage. Just when he was done re-imagining the mass as a Cirque du Soleil production, with angels descending from wires, the parish took their seats.

*"I am confident of this, that the one who began a good work in you will continue to complete it until the day of Christ Jesus."*

Father Sam started his homily from the vestibule. He was thin and looked tired. If not for the clerical collar, he would blend into any crowd. There was nothing remarkable about the silver-haired man, except the subtle Creole accent that seemed misplaced coming out of an otherwise Irish man.

"In our first reading, Paul reminds us that we are mere vessels for God's great purpose and that our confidence and trust must remain not in ourselves, but in Him."

Clay noticed that the more passionate the man became, the stronger his Creole accent revealed itself. He was confident that he spent years working with the poor in New Orleans. For him, this hidden history from an otherwise unremarkable man was all the credibility he needed.

Reaching for an offering envelope and miniature pencil, he began scribbling away. He had learned a trade secret from all those years on set: namely, how writers and producers recycled storylines from other popular shows. In fact, the writers were always reading through other scripts, finding ways to tweak a concept just enough to fit the show and not result in legal action. By the end of the run, the writers were actually tweaking storylines they had already done in earlier seasons. Clay hated the practice, engaging in legendary arguments that halted production, but had recently grown to appreciate its merits.

"We must get out of the way, and let God work in and through us," the priest said emphatically.

Clay wrote as fast as he could, his fingers cramping from the miniature pencil. Soon the offering envelope was covered with his plagiarized notes. He found his answer. He wasn't going to disappoint anyone, not Reagan, not Becky, and, especially, not Tyler. Whatever the outcome, they would at least know that he tried, even if "technically" he was "re-purposing" another guy's message. But that was beside the point. This was for the greater good, so he was willing to bet God wouldn't nail him on a technicality, right? For once he was a happy man.

# Chapter Twenty-Six

"Finally, let me make this clear." The Creole accent was undeniably evident as the Irish priest made his last point with authority.

Clay mouthed Father Sam's words as he wrote, quietly mimicking his Creole accent. "Finally, let me make this clear."

"There are *no short cuts* in this work God has called you to do."

"There are *no short cuts*...." Clay looked up from scribbling as the words slowly sunk in.

"It is a charge that no one can do for you. You must do it for yourself!"

If not for the authority in his voice, Clay might have ignored the warning, but this old priest had gotten the better of him.

Conviction washed over Clay's face.

Reaching into his pocket, he pulled out a crumpled five-dollar bill. He stuffed it into his note-covered envelope and sealed it, along with his fate, tossing it into the offering basket as the usher approached.

The elderly woman beside him noticed what he had done. She whispered in bewilderment, "But you took such good notes."

He watched as his last best hope made its way down the aisle in a wire basket.

The mass ended, although a few parishioners slipped out after taking communion. Clay remained in the pew, devastated. He was out of options, and he knew it. He didn't know what to do. Should he run or tell Reagan he couldn't do it?

The elderly woman, who stayed behind, could tell he was troubled. She took a dollar bill out from her purse. Standing up, she patted him on the head. "I'll light you a candle."

All he felt was the disappointment of everyone he would be letting down. It was a familiar feeling that always overwhelmed him. As much as he tried, he couldn't get Tyler's disappointed face out of his mind; the same look must have been on Bella's face every time she remembered his broken promise to her.

He glanced at the illuminated votives in the distance: red and gold glass on one side and blue and white on the other. They were the glimmering prayers of hope.

There was only one other thing he could do, but he was unsure if he had it in him, unsure if it would work. It's what Reagan was betting on all along.

Rose must have told him how I used to wait for the words to come, how the voice used to speak to me. But Reagan doesn't know how much I've changed in these years, how callous a bruised spirit can become when everything that was unacknowledged remains swept under the rug. What he wants is for me to go inside and I can't go there. I don't know what I'd hear if I did, or worse yet, if I'd be able to get back.

Reluctantly, Clay pulled his burnt leather journal out of his backpack. He untied the knot from the rope around it and opened it. His own handwriting, his heart poured out before his eyes. Memories from a lifetime ago, finally seeing the light of day. The distance time put in place was now erased.

He read the inscription on the inside cover.

*"To Clay: The right words at the right time can change everything. I believe. Rose Mitchell."*

He watched as the woman made her way down the side aisle and lit the candle, the flickering flame melting the hardened wax.

\*

"He can't write something like this! Did you bring him here to make a fool out of me?" Ted pleaded with his father. "How do you even know he has a relationship with God?"

"I'm betting that if he doesn't, he will by the time he writes the message," Reagan said.

"Your belief in him is overwhelming." Ted had fought his whole life for such confidence from his father. The moment he thought he had it, he realized it had slipped through his fingers. "The church is going to know I didn't write it. Have you considered the damage when people find out?"

"I'm prepared for the fallout should that occur."

Ted picked up a Bible from his father's desk and waved it. "What translation are you reading because I don't recall a former-child-star protection program in here?"

"Careful how you wave that book, Theodore. It's supposed to be Good News."

"You're hiding him. How do you justify that?"

"The woman caught in adultery: Jesus didn't humiliate her. He protected her. God doesn't expose people. He covers them with grace. Ted, you know this."

Ted glanced at the Bible in his hand.

"I know that isn't the church I built, but it is what we must become. A hospital for sinners."

"And we're starting with Clay?" Ted said.

"What is it that you object to? That he may not be able to write it or that I'm giving the boy a chance?"

Ted struggled to look past his own resentment.

"He is more like you than you know," Reagan said. "That boy carried the weight of the world on his shoulders. And the people who handled him, well, they were not kind. Ted, you do remember, don't you?"

Ted started to remember.

"The signs were all there that summer," Reagan said. "For some memories only the passing of time reveals their significance."

All Ted recalled was that one afternoon. He hadn't given it much thought in years.

*Reagan and Rose were already at the stadium. Ted had*

*stayed behind. He sat on the hotel bed working on his college applications, self-conscious of the bright abstinence T-shirt he was wearing that read: "I'm not doin' it!"*

*He was reviewing the corrections his father had made to his essay when he heard yelling in the hallway. "You little shit! You've done it now!"*

*Fixing his eyes on the page, he tried to concentrate but the voice grew louder.*

*"You're dead! When I get my hands on you!"*

*Ted was startled when the adjoining door burst open.*

*Clay sprang into the room, quickly shutting the door as he caught his breath. He glanced at Ted across the room. "Nice T-shirt."*

*"What do you think you're doing?"*

*"I'm just passing through." Clay moved to the front door, opened it briefly, and then promptly shut it. "Correction, I'm hiding!"*

*"There is a stadium of kids waiting to see you. They're going to sing happy birthday and everything."*

*"It's a bitch being a kid. The sooner they find that out the better."*

*The voice in the hallway grew louder. "You little shit! I swear, when I find you..."*

*Desperate, Clay searched for a place to hide. After a moment, he crawled under the bed Ted was sitting on.*

*"You can't—" Ted objected, wanting no part in this mess.*

*"Preacher kid, help a guy out."*

*"My name is Ted."*

*Clay stuck his head out from under the bed, his eyes revealing the seriousness of the situation. "Ted. Cover for me.*

*Please, hide me."*

*Ted saw the fear in his eyes.*

*The adjoining door burst open, just as Clay slid back under the bed, his terrified eyes betraying the darkness of the hidden space.*

"That man who was always with him."

"Burt."

"Clay begged me not to say anything." The realization became so clear. Waves of guilt washed over Ted. "I didn't know. I didn't protect him."

"Nobody did."

"That was a long time ago. We were kids. That doesn't give you the right to make a fool out of me now."

Reagan put his hand on his son's shoulder. "Ted, nobody protected him."

✳

The golden rays poured in through the stained glass windows, warming the side of Clay's face, but he barely noticed.

The church was empty. He sat there in the wooden pew, the opened journal beside him, staring blankly into the distance as the words seeped in. He felt safe in the stillness, safe enough to listen.

When he was younger he used to wait for the words to come. He would return to the backlot after dark, finding refuge atop the rusty scaffolding behind the façade-lined streets. He would write into the early morning hours, in a time when God still spoke to him and the words came easily. But as time passed, he was never still long enough for the words to arrive.

Now in the sacred silence he waited like he had done when he was a boy, with an open mind, heart and spirit. But the only words that came to him were the ones given the night of the fire.

*...scared children—all of us—dealing with adult things— wondering if we are that strong. And everyone wants us to be someone or something else.*

Those words had returned to him numerous times in the years that followed but he always resisted letting them in. They were a link to his past and an unfortunate truth that he knew he could do nothing about. They made him feel helpless and he hated that.

Here he was now, opening himself up, desperately waiting for a new word, but the same phrase repeated in his spirit, each time accompanied by a flood of memories that threatened to overwhelm him.

*...scared children—all of us—dealing with adult things— wondering if we are that strong. And everyone wants us to be someone or something else.*

He was no longer alone in the church. The accusing faces and voices from his youth filled the pews around him. He should have known better than to open this door to the past.

Staring at the illuminated candles located throughout the church, he was curious if all prayers were answered in this way or maybe just his prayers? He didn't exactly blame God for not speaking to him anymore. He just didn't understand what he was supposed to do, what God expected from him.

All Clay knew was what he didn't want and at the top of that list was feeling this junk again. What was the purpose? If not for his bum shoulder, a few scars on his body or the way he instinctively cowered when he heard a sudden noise, he may have convinced himself that nothing ever happened. Or worse yet, whatever did occur he had brought upon himself.

It was amazing how incredibly confusing everything could get, how uncertain the certain could become.

"Maybe they were right? Maybe they were all right?"

His angry eyes rose above the flickering flames that surrounded him. He realized that along the walls, to the right and left of him, were ceramic interpretations of the paintings he discovered in the barn, each unjust moment memorialized in Spanish glazed tile. He had been sitting in the midst of them the whole time and hadn't even noticed.

Clay wondered who had commissioned the hidden paintings displayed in the hallways of his own mind. He hated to admit it but that stuff was always with him and always around him.

He thought about running but where would he go?

He had been willing to open up, wait for the words to come, but these memories were all he got. He tried to tell himself that he didn't care, that this wasn't his problem and that he had been brought here under false pretenses. But the feelings wouldn't dissipate. He just kept picturing Tyler's face.

Clay stared at the gilded crucifix above the altar; it was Hope taking its last breath.

After a few moments, he noticed Father Sam walk down the aisle and go into the confessional. From the pew, he watched the green light turn on.

# Chapter Twenty-Seven

Clay took a deep breath, opened the confessional door and hesitated, surprised by the setup. It didn't look like it did in the movies. The intimate room resembled a counseling office with two chairs facing each other. This was one modern improvement he could have done without.

He couldn't believe he was going through with this. Calm down. How hard can this be? Fess up, get yelled at, and get out.

Father Sam was not making eye contact, so Clay crossed the threshold and eased into the seat. He was intrigued by the man and thought about talking to him, but now inside, he felt the gravity of what this was all about.

Clay had played a dyslexic Irish orphan named Scully on a Network Afternoon Special called *"Not Without My Slingshot"* with George Hamilton as the neighborhood priest. Admittedly, it was a stretch for both of them. But in this moment he would have done anything to confess Scully's sins instead. Maybe I can excuse myself, buy a slingshot, break a window and come back? One thing is certain, honesty is easier when you're playing a character and the priest chastising you is a man with a tan. But this is the real thing, and Father Sam is obviously not a sun dweller.

"In the name of the Father, Son and Holy Spirit."

Lowering his head, Clay struggled to discern his own thoughts from the accusing voices that had filled the church on the other side of the door.

Father Sam waited in the silence. "Have you done something?"

"Well, when I was a teenager I did start a fire that burned down a Hollywood studio backlot."

Father Sam couldn't help but look up.

"It was an accident, and, trust me, I've been paying for it ever since."

The priest lowered his gaze again.

"A lot of people lost their jobs. Families were hurt. It ruined my mom's life, too." Clay paused. "Even though it was an accident, the truth is I wanted it to happen. Not for the studio to burn, but for it to all go away, for that part of my life to end. The truth is I wanted it." Clay ran his fingers through his hair. "Of all the prayers I prayed, I didn't know that would be the one God would answer."

"What else?"

Clay sorted through his sins, all the illegitimate ways he tried to meet his legitimate needs. He searched for the ugliest one beneath them all. They seemed endless. The remorse was real—*very real*—but it didn't bring relief.

"There are plenty of things I'm not proud of—the fire, the tantrums, the women, all the self-centered choices I'm famous for—but it's more than that." Waves of shame and fear flooded in like a riptide sweeping him out to sea. He could no longer touch the ocean floor or swim safely to shore. Clay tried to put his finger on it and he just couldn't. "I'm just sorry. I'm just always sorry."

The priest pressed him again. "Sorry for *what*?"

Clay looked up in frustration. "I'm sorry I'm me."

Father Sam glanced up.

Even Clay was surprised by what he had blurted out. "I am. I think I always have been. I don't know how else to explain it." Clay felt a strange mix of shame and relief. Suddenly his question had become so clear. "I don't know how this thing works, but can you do that?"

"Do what?"

"Can you absolve me for being me?"

"You want me to absolve you for being you?" The silver-haired man gazed at him in disbelief. Father Sam recognized the desperation in his eyes.

"What's the use of being forgiven when you're the problem?" Clay paused. "You think if you could just change the things you do, the things you've done, that it will make the difference. It never does. It's hard, holding yourself together, when so many of those pieces are, *flawed*. And you start to turn on yourself in so many little ways. You get really tired of disappointing people."

"I see." The priest lowered his head, but Clay interrupted him.

"One more thing. I'm not Catholic."

"You're not Catholic?"

"There is this kid I made a promise to, and I just thought

that if I did this, God might relent and let me not disappoint him. Besides, I needed my pipes cleaned. And I trust you."

"You may not be Catholic, but I am still going to give you penance." Father Sam's voice was surprisingly stern. "You do know what penance is, right?"

Clay nodded yes, convinced he'd been paying it most of his life.

"Confession is serious business. You have offended God, and He doesn't take that lightly. Are you ready?"

Tightening his body, Clay stared at the ground, waiting for the punishment he knew he had coming. His posture was not unlike when he knew Burt was about to unleash his anger, or indulge in his perversion. A brutal beating could bring relief, temporarily removing the threat while quenching Burt's wrath. He had endured those countless times before. But that was only Burt, not God.

Clay caught his breath, waiting for the swing of the bat.

"This is your penance. You are to spend the remainder of this day envisioning God Himself repeating these words to you: 'You are my beloved son, in whom I am well pleased'."

Clay lifted his head, wondering if he heard the priest correctly.

"You are my beloved son, in whom I am well pleased."

Father Sam's voice echoed in Clay's mind as the words seeped in. The phrase was challenging every other voice he had been convinced was true.

He closed his eyes to concentrate, but could only see the hidden paintings from his youth: the collection of moments that led up to the night of the fire.

*Through that blurry, rain-soaked window, Clay screamed, watching his mother get on the bus. He had tried to follow, but felt a hand on his shoulder holding him back.* "No!" *He screamed louder, his objection fogging up the glass.* "No!"

"You are my beloved son, in whom I am well pleased."
His eyes filled with tears. He raised his head, looking directly at Father Sam.

*Clay walked off the stage. A callous hand grabbed him, throwing him up against the wall. He felt his head slam against the brick, the man's stale breath in his face, his shoulder throbbing where it had been dislocated before.*

"You are my beloved son, in whom I am well pleased."
Clay cried, a part of him wanting to believe, another wanting the priest to shut up.

*Clay lost his grip on the banister as the man's forearm pushed against his chest. He tried to brace himself as he fell backwards, his body tumbling down the stairwell.*

"You are my beloved son, in whom I am well pleased."

*The flash of the camera illuminated his bare body. With terrified eyes, he had no voice to scream, no strength to fight back, the figure of a man towering over him. The second flash of the camera.*

"You are my beloved son, in whom I am well pleased."

*Clay's face basked in the orange glow of the blaze, staring blankly into the fire. He watched as the plastic Halloween mask slowly melted.*

"You are my beloved son, in whom I am well pleased."

Sobbing, tears flowed from a place deep within, a place Clay hadn't accessed since his youth. Wiping the tears from his face, he realized that the mask was gone that night, but what was underneath still needed to be healed.

"It's true. You can believe it." Father Sam leaned forward. "Sometimes it's too much. Our emotions, our minds, our bodies, they just can't take it. God knows His children get scared. *Sin is sin*, but it's okay to be human. You don't have to apologize for that.

"There's a difference between doing something bad and believing you are bad. God did not create you to hate yourself. God will not compete with a false perception of Himself. Everything you've done. Everyone who hurt you, these are false gods you must stop worshiping. He created you in His image and you offend Him when you don't see yourself in that light. It takes courage to believe that you are the beloved of God."

"But what if..." Tears dripped from Clay's eyes, his body trembling as he tried to catch his breath. "But what if I can't change how I feel?"

"It can be hard to believe we'll ever get well, especially when we see our wounds for what they really are. Don't be ashamed of your wounds. Remember they become scars bringing healing to others."

Father Sam pulled a box of Kleenex from under his chair

and handed it to Clay.

"This is hard stuff. But you're getting honest—*confessing your part*, and He's meeting you where you are right now, dusting off the sin and everything that has made us *less* human. And once more we begin to believe, we see Him, and we see ourselves for who we really are: beloved children of God.

"Go in peace," the priest added.

Rising, through his sincere eyes, Clay silently thanked the priest. Opening the confessional door, he exhaled as if a heavy weight had been lifted off his very being.

Clay squinted from the bright sun as he exited the church, somehow embarrassed that he had gotten so emotional.

The priest had been very kind but was Clay really going to spend the rest of the afternoon repeating that phrase in his head? He found that in spite of himself, he did just that.

He felt ridiculous, walking around town, telling himself that he was beloved but he did it anyhow.

He said it as he passed the Cliff Falls Library and again when he reached the town square.

He said it as he sat on a bench in the park, watching the children play on the playground.

"You are my beloved son, in whom I am well pleased."

He said it again and again and again.

And each time he did, the vivid memories and accusing voices returned, but he just kept repeating it, allowing the words to enter his spirit and permeate him in an unexpected way.

Soon he wasn't repeating it anymore, he was hearing it.

And it wasn't his own voice; it was another, one more tender.

"You are my beloved son, in whom I am well pleased."

As people passed him on the street, he pictured God saying it to them. "You are my beloved daughter. You are my beloved son."

The voice was so strong, he wondered if they could hear it.

He stopped by the Acorn, but didn't go inside. He just glanced at the counter, seeing it as Becky did, and in the painted faces in the mural overhead.

"You are my beloved son, in whom I am well pleased."

*"Scared children—all of us—dealing with adult things—wondering if we are that strong. And everyone wants us to be someone or something else, but...you are my beloved son, in whom I am well pleased."* He shook his head. It was the rest of the phrase.

Clay made his way up the rustic trail, the words repeating in his spirit. He noticed the magnificent oaks that lined his path. In the stillness, he listened to the quiet rustling of leaves as he continued along the trail. Soon he came upon the rushing falls the city was named for. Three separate falls emanating from one source. The sight was majestic.

Light filtered through the golden oak leaves above the rushing waters. Standing on a rock, he could see his shadow on the opposite bank of the river. The roar of the water plunging over the cliff; the outflow emptying into the river, cascading over the falls. Everything he was carrying was being swept away. The mighty roar was consuming him. The mighty roar was calling out his name.

"You are my beloved son, in whom I am well pleased."

The falls made everything come alive. He breathed in deeply. It was as if he were taking his first breath.

By the time the sun had set, something had changed. He had changed.

Clay sat on that rock looking over the falls, the moon illuminating the rushing water. He removed his journal from his backpack, opened the last pages, the only ones blank, and began to write.

*"The falls are flowing through me now. It's like I've sunk deep beneath the water, gasping for air, but came up the other side. It wasn't safe. It wasn't supposed to be. But I'm all right, and I'm not alone. I don't know which was more frightening: God or life?*

*"When you're underneath, you're alone, and it's scary and for a few moments, unbearable. But then you emerge, and you're all right and somehow changed. The transformation that eluded me, like all observers who stand on the banks, is finally here."*

Suddenly it became so clear to Clay.

*"Knowing who you are not, is always the beginning of change; but until you hear your true name, you will wander, and perhaps, all should for a time."*

Clay continued writing as he listened to the sound of the rushing water.

✳

Clay made it back to town. He sat at the counter at the Acorn, thinking. His journal full, he leaned over to borrow paper from a teenager doing homework at a nearby table. She was out of paper, so he started writing on a napkin.

He spent the rest of the evening writing.

Returning to his church campus apartment, he turned the light on and then placed a borrowed laptop labeled "Property of Max. Do not remove!" on his desk.

After turning it on, he began removing scraps of paper—napkins, and a few placemats—from his pocket, the sum of which comprised his message.

Clay was deep in thought. He passionately transferred his message into the laptop from the scraps that lined his desk. After a moment, he stopped to relish in the quiet pride of something he wrote. He had found the words that resonated and the place from which they flowed.

Now to find a printer.

✳

Lots were cast worldwide as the bidding wars raged on.

| | | | | |
|---|---|---|---|---|
| "'Little Guy Mike' Halloween mask" | $262 | 1d | 0h | 10m |
| "TV Guide featuring Clay on the cover" | $165 | 2d | 3h | 4m |
| "LGM Jacket worn by Clay" | $200 | 5d | 13h | 22m |
| "'Little Guy Mike' Microphone" | $23 | 6d | 2h | 14m |

Ted stared at the computer screen in his office, unable to understand why the world still cared so much about Clay

Grant. Nor could he understand why Clay fought so hard against it.

He sat there feeling sorry that he didn't recognize the signs of abuse all those years ago; but he was a kid with his own problems. Why should his reputation be at risk just so his father could assuage his guilt?

Ted stared out his office window. What did his father see in Clay? Reagan was always too busy for Ted. For as hard as Ted always tried to gain his father's support, Clay had it effortlessly. Maybe he did envy him, but the guy had everything, and now he even had his father.

*

A solitary figure strolled across the vast church campus lawn. Clay stopped at Ted's office noticing that the light was on. He slipped the message under the door. Walking away, he couldn't help but feel good about what he had accomplished.

*

Clay was already in bed when he heard the first knock at his door. It was amazing how fast a newfound peace could be disturbed. He thought about ignoring it, but it persisted. Turning on the lamp, he got up and opened the door.

Ted was seething. Waving Clay's sermon in his hand, he shouted, "What gives you the right?"

Clay didn't follow. Ted's anger seemed out of proportion for what Clay tried to convey. "I just tried to write something that was honest. People can't relate to an image of perfection. Trust me, I know."

"I've given this church everything: my childhood, my parents, my life. I'm not giving them this!"

"What are you talking about?"

"I'd go to my father but I know he'd just back you up." There was desperation in his eyes. "So I'm appealing to you, hoping something inside your selfish being will do the right thing."

"The right thing?"

"I'll get you whatever cash you need. I don't care if I have to mortgage my house. But I want you gone by morning."

"What did I do wrong?"

"As far as we are concerned, you never wrote this."

"And if I don't leave?"

"Don't force my hand."

The threat didn't go unnoticed. Normally, Clay would have been out the door, but something inside of him had changed. He was proud of what he had written and was not going to be run off so easily.

"If you've been dealt such a raw deal, why don't you leave?" Clay said.

"Because some people live with the choices they make, even if they can't remember when or where they made them. They can't afford to be reckless because people depend upon them. But what would you know about that? By the time the impact hits, you're a hundred miles away."

"I'm done living like that. I know who I am now and I don't care what you or anyone else has to say about it."

"This isn't just about you! You have no idea what's at

stake here."

"Don't tell me you believe what Tyler does?" Clay said with sarcasm.

"What's that?"

"That if you do a really good job, your wife is going to come back."

"I pray every day that she never comes back."

It was a stunning admission. Clay stared at Ted in confusion.

"Because I know if she does, it will only be to take Tyler with her. He's all I have. This lousy church is all I have." Ted pleaded with him. "If I look like a fool, I will lose everything."

"You really expect me to leave?"

"What's the difference? At some point you're just going to run anyhow. That's what you do. That's what you've always done, isn't it?"

Clay stood there silent.

"For once in your life, do something selfless. Go. Now." Ted crumpled the paper still in his hand. "I'm begging you. Leave this place."

# *Chapter Twenty-Eight*

Becky wrote the daily specials on the chalkboard, playfully decorating the perimeter with happy, yellow chalk sunflowers.

"He bakes?" one of Becky's co-workers said.

"He used to work in an Italian bakery. We already have our first official date planned out, should that occur. He's going to teach me how to make authentic pastries: Tiramisu, biscotti..."

"What's wrong with our Tiramisu?" She pointed to the California-version in the pastry case.

"Clay says that you never know you've got the fake thing, unless you've had the real thing."

"Sounds like a cola commercial."

"That's what I said. Apparently, one bite of an authentic Italian pastry and I won't be able to look at that other stuff again. The real thing is supposed to change my life."

"Sounds like it already has."

Amid the crowd, a man sat at the counter eating

a sandwich.

The waitress approached him. "Will that be all?"

Burt looked up as he chewed the last of his sandwich.

"Excuse me?" Burt said. "I can see the church from the street. Can you tell me what road I take to get up there?"

Becky pointed out the window. "You just follow Ridge Road all the way up."

\*

Clay was almost packed. Placing the last of his clothes in his duffel bag, he zipped it. He couldn't get past it. He had done everything they asked him to do and he was still being sent away.

He stayed up half the night deciding whether to stay for Reagan or leave for Ted, but as the sun emerged over the hillside his choice became clear. Why was it that for Clay, the selfless thing to do was to disappear?

Putting on his backpack, he took one last look around, the twin bed, nightstand, and the bare desk beneath the vast window where he composed his message. He was going to miss this place. Glancing at the old television set with aluminum-covered rabbit ears, Clay shook his head.

He had written Reagan a letter but decided not to leave it. He didn't want to cause any more problems, so he just slipped it into his backpack. It was better for everyone if they just assumed that he ran, better for everyone that was, except for Clay.

Moving to the window, Clay looked out over the mountainous landscape, staring at that babbling creek before turning to leave.

\*

Reagan was coming up the steps to Clay's apartment, hoping to get a preview of what he had composed. It wasn't that he doubted him; he just wanted to look it over before Ted. He thought he could help smooth out any rough spots or Biblical inconsistencies. He went to knock on the door but realized that it was open.

Stepping inside, he found it empty. There was not a trace of Clay anywhere.

Reagan blamed himself. Obviously he had expected too much of the boy, thinking he could write it, and that drove him off. What had he done? Everything he had set in motion would unravel. If ever Reagan needed Rose it was now.

As he turned to leave, he noticed the trash pail beside the bare desk. It was filled with scraps of paper, each one covered in hand-written scribbling. Crouching down, Reagan read through the scraps.

\*

Diego and a crew were busy working among the thorny shrubs in the memorial garden installing the last section of the wrought iron gate along the perimeter. It was hot and the work was physical. He was sweating and catching his breath when he noticed a man taking pictures of the property. As the crew took a break, Diego walked over to the man.

"Afternoon," Diego said, wiping the sweat from his brow.

"They sell postcards in the gift shop."

Burt lowered his camera. He was cautious not to ask just anyone. He didn't want to tip Clay off. "This is such a beautiful church. It would be a shame if something happened to it."

Diego looked at him bewildered.

"Do you watch much television?"

Burt showed him the picture of Clay covered in flour. "It's blurry, but you get the idea. 'Little Guy Mike'. He was one of the biggest stars on TV. Have you seen him?"

✳

Ted glanced at the message on the desk, trying to justify what he had done the night before. He hadn't expected for it to affect him so deeply. It had become too personal to him. It was like Clay was in his head.

He wondered if Clay had actually left, but then he heard his father and Tyler in the corridor. His heart raced.

"He's gone, Dad. He's gone."

Reagan didn't have to ask. Ted's guilt-ridden face gave him away.

"I know," Ted said quietly.

Tyler stared at his father in bewilderment. "Why would he leave? He promised."

Reagan held his tongue.

"I'll explain everything to you later," Ted said. "Right now, I need to talk to your grandfather."

"He didn't even say goodbye," Tyler said.

"He had to leave in a hurry," Ted replied.

"Everyone around here leaves in a hurry!" Tyler left

disappointed.

Reagan waited for the boy to leave. "I won't stand for you running him off. What did you say to him?"

Ted picked up the message on the desk. "Did you read this?"

Reagan looked away.

"You'll go to any length to make sure Clay isn't exploited, but me—"

"You don't understand."

"Just say it. You have no confidence in me."

"That's not true."

"No, it is true. My words. My voice. They have never been enough. I've never been enough."

"You can't see it now but I am doing this for you. I am for you, not against you. Son, I need you to believe that."

Ted was not convinced.

"Sending Clay off, I know this is not the man you want to be. This is not the example you want to set for Tyler." Reagan knew they were wasting time. "You can change this. Be the better man."

"That's the problem. The Great Reagan Mitchell. I've never been the better man." Ted stared blankly out the window, his father's reflection visible in the glass.

"You were that night." Reagan leaned in. "When your mother passed, I looked for any excuse to leave. Ted, she was my strength, and the moment she was gone, my strength was gone. I couldn't face you or anyone else. So I ran. But not you. You stayed.

"It's a sad moment, when you finally have need for all that you've been preaching, my special brand of inspiration, and find it wholly inadequate. That's a scary place to be."

"Why him?"

"Helping Clay wasn't my idea. It was your mother's."
Reagan stared at his son's reflection in the glass. "You are so much like her. I just want everyone to see that."

Ted felt betrayed. "It was mom's idea?"

\*

Diego held the blurry photograph in his hand, staring at the green eyes.

"I'm telling you, he's trouble. I know. He destroys everything in his path."

Burt handed him others, pictures of Clay disguised in sunglasses, a knit hat.

"What makes you think he'd be here?"

"He loves the mountains, the open space. Probably from all those years cooped up in a studio. Besides, I have a reliable tip."

Diego handed Burt back his pictures.

"Someone is helping him. If he's not in Cliff Falls now, he was."

Burt pulled his wallet out and removed a few hundred-dollar bills. "You're sure you haven't seen him?"

Diego refused the money. "I haven't seen the man you describe. I can tell you that for certain."

"If he does show up, I hope you have good fire insurance," Burt said.

Burt handed Diego his card. "Call me if you hear anything and I'll make it worth your trouble."

Burt took a few more photographs before making his way

back down the hill.

*

The bell on the door jingled as Clay stepped into the diner. Once again he was carrying his duffel bag. It was against his better judgment but he knew he couldn't leave without saying goodbye. He owed it to her but he just didn't know if he could go through with it. He grasped his duffel bag as the door slowly shut. This was the point of no return.

Becky was working the counter. She had just finished taking an order when she looked up and noticed him. It took her a moment but she had seen this scene before.

Clay stood there speechless.

"Let me guess, Tiramisu and a phonebook?" Becky caught herself. "What am I thinking? Scratch the Tiramisu; just the phonebook."

He couldn't even look at her.

She retrieved the yellow pages from under the counter and dropped it on the table next to him.

Clay couldn't help but glance at the glossy picture of the rushing falls on the cover, for a moment forgetting he had stumbled upon the real falls the day before and the change that he was certain was lasting. The disappointment was devastating. He looked at her, speechless, knowing that his best of intentions were never good enough, especially when he was the problem.

Becky waited for him to say something, anything. But there was just silence. "That's all right," she said quietly, "I know how hard it is for you to find the words."

She turned to walk away, angry with herself for not knowing better, for allowing herself to get that close to him.

"Becky..."

She hesitated, hoping for words other than what was spoken.

"I'm sorry."

Becky turned to the other waitress. "Cover for me."

The waitress nodded.

Becky held back tears as she walked out of the door.

Clay didn't run after her. He just stood there frozen. It was better for her to hate him. He couldn't show it but this was killing him. He watched as she left the diner.

Reaching into his pocket, Clay pulled out a dollar and turned to the waitress. "Can I get some change? I need to call a cab."

She looked at him with contempt.

"Never mind."


Parking his car along Ridge Road, Ted was wondering where to begin looking when he spotted Clay through the plate glass window of the Acorn Diner. He took a deep breath before stepping inside.

Clay felt the anger well up inside of him when he noticed Ted in the doorway.

"Look, I owe you an apology," Ted said, as he approached him.

"I can't do this."

"I'm apologizing here."

"It doesn't matter now. You're too late," Clay said, thinking of Becky. "You were right. This was a mistake."

Clay turned to leave, but remembered the letter he had written Reagan was in his backpack. He hadn't planned to leave it, but now that Ted was here, it would give him closure. Slipping off his backpack, he unzipped it and retrieved the letter. "Do me a favor. Give this to your father and tell him thank you."

Ted took the folded letter.

"In fact, thank everyone for me." He paused, smiling. "Especially Diego. He's a good man."

Clay reached for his duffel bag. "And Tyler. Just tell him he was right. A church isn't a very good hiding place."

Clay took one last look around, glancing at the watchful faces in the mural overhead. He had just started to believe there might be a place for him at the counter.

As he turned to leave, Clay knew he had to tell Ted the truth. "For the record, that message wasn't about you. It was about me."

Ted stood in that diner overwhelmed, the folded letter in his hand. Even if he really wanted to, Ted didn't know how to make him stay. He never knew how to make people stay.

The bell on the door jingled as Clay walked out of the diner.

Ted wavered but he needed to know what Clay had written to his father. Unfolding the letter, he settled into a booth beside the window facing Cliff Falls Drive and quickly became engrossed.

*"Until you showed up, I never knew I was waiting to be found."*

Ted was surprised.

"And you didn't come after 'Little Guy Mike'. You came after me. I guess I've been waiting my whole life for someone to come after me."

Ted stared at the hand-written letter, finally understanding what his father had done.

Clay was on foot making his way down Cliff Falls Drive. He spotted a pay phone at the gas station. Reaching into his pocket for a dollar, Clay approached the gas station attendant.

"Can I get some change?"

"You'll have to go inside."

Clay walked to the cashier's window. As he approached, he saw Burt paying for gas.

Panicking, Clay gripped his duffel bag, turned, and raced back towards the church.

Ted glanced out the window and saw him. He got up from the booth and ran outside. He called out to him. "Clay!"

Clay stopped in his tracks. Visibly shaken, he looked at Ted. "Burt's here!"

Ted recognized the fear in his eyes. It was the same fear from all those years ago. As he clutched the letter in his hand, Ted said, "Let me get you out of here."

# Chapter Twenty-Nine

Ted swung open the weathered barn door. "I didn't know where else to take him."

Reagan stepped inside as Ted closed the door. Dust kicked up as the light seeped in through the splintered wood. It had been years since Reagan had set foot inside the old barn.

His eyes were distracted by the canvases that lined the walls. He had known of Diego's artwork, but these paintings were mesmerizing. He couldn't take his eyes off them. This ramshackle barn felt holier than the church he'd built.

Ted called out for Clay but he was nowhere to be found.

Reagan stared at the weary eyes in the paintings. "We shouldn't have left him by himself."

"He couldn't have gotten far. I'll find him. I promise." Ted turned to leave.

"Wait," his father said quietly, turning his attention away from the paintings. He called out for Clay.

Responding to Reagan's voice, Clay emerged from the

upper rafters.

Ted exhaled.

"How did he find you?" Reagan said. "I took every precaution to protect you."

Clay glanced at Ted below.

The accusation did not go unnoticed. Reagan looked at his son having not considered the option.

"I swear it wasn't me." Ted needed them to believe him. "Whatever our differences, you have to know I wouldn't do that."

Clay couldn't figure out how else Burt could have found him. He tossed his bags below and climbed down the wooden ladder.

"Don't do anything rash," Reagan said.

"Fishing boats go in and out of Half Moon Bay, right?"

"I believe so," Ted responded.

"I can hike through the mountain pass, blend in with all the other hikers, and make it there by nightfall."

"It doesn't make sense to try to leave now," Reagan insisted. "Just stay the night. If you still want to go in the morning, I promise I won't stop you."

"I know Burt. He's not going away."

Reagan wasn't about to let him go without a fight. "We had a deal."

"You left a few things out of that deal." It was obvious that Clay was referring to Ted.

Ted took a defensive posture. "I just saved your ass."

Reagan interjected. "Please!"

"I am sorry for how your life has turned out, but this is not my fault. Do what you want, but I'm done apologizing." Ted walked away frustrated. He knew he could never win.

"You two have more in common than either of you realize," Reagan said. "You know growing up under a microscope does something to a boy. It can stifle his voice."

"You bet on the wrong guy. I'm not Old Ironsides. Why can't you see that?"

"We're leaky, wooden vessels, Clay. That's all we are meant to be. The only words that matter are the ones that flow from the cracks in our spirit, through the breaches in our resolve. I wish I had known that all those years ago."

Clay saw himself in the tortured paintings as he planned his escape.

"Tell me, Clay, how does a man change something he's spent a life creating? A church? A son?"

"I can't do this."

"You already have. I read what you wrote."

"You don't get it. I'm not safe. Burt is probably on his way back here right now. By tomorrow, my face could be plastered on every media network across the globe. You have no idea what I've done trying to find an ounce of peace. What I've done trying to reclaim every fragment of myself that is out there, every missing piece that I'll never get back. But that doesn't matter now. Nothing I do matters!" Clay stared at the canvases, the tortured portraits of Jesus that surrounded him. "I can't escape it!"

"I'm going to let you in on a secret," Reagan said. "Rose was right. No one escapes it. No one escapes life."

"It doesn't matter what I do. It will always be the same. My life will always feel like some cancelled television pilot."

"Until you stop running that's true; another city, another

girl, another new beginning. It's important to stay, to get to the middle. That's where life happens. Right now everything has promise, but until you decide to stay, that's all it will ever be. Don't make the same mistake now, like the night of the fire. Don't run."

"I'm sorry. I warned you."

Reagan wouldn't hear it. "Just stay the night. Don't leave this barn. I promise I will take care of this."

Clay gripped his duffel bag.

✳

Ted was several feet outside the barn: in his hand, the letter Clay had written his father. In all the confusion, he had forgotten to give it to Reagan. He glanced over it again, the sentiment fresh in his mind.

*"Until you showed up, I never knew I was waiting to be found...I guess I've been waiting my whole life for someone to come after me."*

The air caught in Ted's chest. Maybe that was the answer? He took his cell phone out and started dialing.

The answering machine played. "Hello, this is Quinn. I'm probably in class right now. Please leave your name and number, and I'll get back to you."

"Quinn, could you give me a call. Tyler misses you. I miss you. I'm not mad anymore."

Quinn picked up the phone. "Ted? I just walked in. Is everything all right? Is Tyler all right?"

"Yeah, he's fine. I've been thinking about you, about us. I want to see you," he said, the letter pressed in his hand. "I'm taking the red eye tonight."

"Aren't you preaching in the morning?"

"I don't care about that anymore. I don't." He took a deep breath, preparing his next move. "I'm coming for you." Ted waited in the awkwardness of the silence.

She cleared her throat on the other end. There was a long pause. "That's not a good idea." Her voice was small but strong. "Not now." She paused again. "I know you are having a hard time Ted but I can't do this anymore."

"But I thought that this is what you wanted." Ted's shoulders slumped.

"I did," she paused, "but that was a long time ago. I need to figure out what I want now. I hope you understand."

"Yeah, I understand." Ted hung up.

✳

Becky unlocked the door to her studio apartment and tossed the keys onto the coffee table beside the wilted sunflowers. She had made it back to the Acorn to finish her shift but the other waitresses told her to go home and that they would cover for her. Even the senior waitresses offered to split their tips. Becky thought she was holding it together but her eyes gave her away.

The red light flashed on the answering machine. As long as Becky didn't answer it, she could hope it was an explanation. It wasn't like she had known him that long, but his sudden departure made her question her instincts and her instincts were one of the few things left that she thought she could trust. That was why she didn't regret that she didn't tell him she knew about his past. Because it didn't matter, she knew that wasn't who he was. She wanted to get to know the real Clay.

Becky pressed the button. The message was from her brother, Max, asking her to reconsider relocating with his family. "Hey, Pumpkin. Chicago isn't that cold in the winter. So I'm exaggerating. But we want you to come. You're not in the way."

Becky glanced at the sunflowers drooping in the glass vase on her coffee table. As the message played, she picked them up and threw them into the trash.

✳

Fog rolled in over the majestic Santa Cruz Mountains as night fell. Clay had been too afraid to step outside, so he just waited up in the rafters with his duffel bag and backpack at his side until it was dark enough for him to leave. Without words, he prayed. He felt like the world was going to consume him.

He stared at the moving fog through an opening in the shingled roof, occasionally catching a glimpse of the star-filled sky.

✳

Ted checked on Tyler, who was asleep in bed. His asthma inhaler, baseball cards and a handheld video game were scattered across the *Dinosaur Kingdom* bed sheets. Placing the items on the nightstand, Ted tucked the blanket around him and kissed him on the forehead.

He went to the closet and took out Tyler's church clothes for the next day, a crisp white shirt, khaki pants and navy striped tie. He hung them on the door.

As Ted turned to leave, Quinn's photo caught his eye. He knew she was done. He turned out the light and shut the door.

\*

The glowing computer monitor illuminated the darkened office. Logging on, a new email was discovered. The subject line read: "Congratulations, you are the highest bidder".

Opening it, the picture of the prize won was enlarged, a rare "Little Guy Mike" Halloween Mask: Price $322.

Scrolling the page, the highest bidder glanced at the seller's name: ClayHeart, Wichita, Kansas, and a link with the familiar instructions: "Contact seller to arrange payment."

Clicking on the seller's link, the highest bidder began to type. "As usual, I will send you a cashier's check. However, I am relocating, so please hold shipment until I forward you a new address."

Staring blankly at the screen, the highest bidder proceeded to shut down the computer, but not before he was surprised by the seller's instant message reply.

"That will be fine. I hope this helps complete your collection. Clay would be happy to know he has such a devoted fan."

Clay rolled his eyes, the Halloween mask obscuring his

reflection in the monitor. Although it was a risk leaving the barn, he needed to take care of business while he still had access to a computer. He glanced at the computer screen clock. It read 11:30 p.m.

"Business must be good if you have to work this late. What time is it, 1:30 in the morning there?"

"I don't mind. I get a lot done this time of night," she typed. "Truth is, work doesn't keep me up as much as it keeps me company."

"May I ask you a personal question?"

"You're my number one buyer. You pay the light bills around here. What's the question?"

Clay always managed to buy a few items a month to help support his mom, scraping together whatever income he made. He was ashamed to admit it, but after all these years, he was still supporting her. She may have abandoned him but for some reason he couldn't do the same. He typed his question.

"What kind of child was Clay?"

"What do you mean?"

"I've read the tabloid stories. I've heard the wild rumors. I've listened to everything everyone has had to say, but this site says that you're his mother, so do you mind if I ask you what kind of child was Clay, really?"

"*Daily Variety* once wrote that when Clay was on the *Bob Hope Christmas Special* he was the only child who could keep up—"

"Before that. Before he went to Hollywood. Was he ever just a kid?"

His mother stared at a photograph on the wall. "Yes, he

was." She and Clay sat high in a tree laughing. They looked young. "We both were."

Clay tried to remember her youthful face. Only now did it occur to him how young she was.

"Back then it was just the two of us," she typed, glancing at the inventory of *Little Guy Mike* auction items surrounding her computer. "Sometimes it still is. People blame Clay, but I wasn't the best mom. You sound like a sincere young man. You must have had a good mom."

"I don't think I realized it at the time," Clay paused, his fingers over the keys, "but she did the best she could."

Staring at the computer monitor, he thought about revealing his identity, but hesitated. One day he might be strong enough to reach out, but for now, this was as close of a connection as he could make.

"May I ask you another question?"

"Sure."

"Do you ever regret leaving him in the hands of his handlers?"

"Every day. And I told one of them that again just the other day."

"What do you mean?"

"This Mr. Cummings came by when I was putting together my packages for the post office. I kept telling him I don't know where Clay is and that I don't want him to keep coming around anymore, but he never listens." She continued typing. "He offered me money, just in case I hear something. But I told him I didn't need it. Not when I have great customers like you supporting me."

"He knows about me?"

"Everyone knows about my highest bidder."

Clay felt a chill race through his body. Burt must have figured it out from the addresses on the boxes. He shouldn't have risked it so soon.

\*

Clay made his way back to the barn, covered in the blanket of night. Opening the weathered door, he stepped inside. There was no light pouring in through the fractured wood now, only darkness.

He tossed his bags in the back of the truck and hopped in the driver's seat. Reaching under the dash, he attempted to cross the wires in the darkness. As the twisted wires made contact, a blinding flash enveloped him. Clenching his eyes, he heard the passenger door open as the engine rumbled.

Turning his head, Clay didn't see a figure, only a lens. The second flash of light.

Clay felt the truck sputter. Pressing on the pedal, he revved the engine, but it was too late. The engine stalled. The third burst of light.

Pulling the door's handle, Clay jumped out of the truck. After retrieving his bags from the bed of the truck, he turned to leave, but he was cornered.

Burt was between Clay and the barn door, readying his camera.

"This is too perfect. It's like our own private session. Just like old times."

Clay held his bags tightly as he backed up in the darkness, trying to fade into the hidden canvases that surrounded him.

Burt aimed his lens into the darkness. "These are going to fetch a mint."

Clay cringed with each shot of the camera; each flash was like a lash against his being.

"You didn't really think you were going to outrun me, did you?"

The hidden paintings—the final hours of Jesus' life—illuminated with each burst of light, a vivid backdrop to each contorted pose. The violent red and purple strokes ignited like fireworks.

Clay couldn't catch his breath. He tried to hold himself together but it was no use. He wished he were stronger but something about being in the presence of this man made him regress. All he knew was that whatever it was that it made him feel, it was the opposite of beloved.

"You know I keep a photo of you in my wallet. It's part of my private collection. Do you want to see it? It reminds me who you really are, weak, pathetic."

Clay dropped his bags. He couldn't escape it.

In the darkness, Clay tripped over his duffel bag and fell to the ground, the flash of the camera brightening the fear in his eyes. Here he was again, helpless.

"Leave him alone," Diego shouted, standing at the entrance of the barn.

Clay looked up.

Burt flashed again.

Diego turned on the truck's headlights, revealing Clay cowering on the ground. "I said, leave him alone."

Clay felt ashamed that Diego saw him like that.

"This is private property," Diego said. "I'm calling the cops."

"Go ahead, call the cops," Burt said, "and then everybody will know where he is."

Diego looked at Clay who had panic in his eyes.

"That's all right. I'm done here." Burt turned to leave.

Diego was between Burt and the door. "Give me the camera."

Burt scoffed at the request.

Diego pushed Burt up against the truck. "I said, give me the camera."

Diego took the camera and, with Burt still pinned against the truck, deleted the images from the memory card. "It's over now."

Burt watched in disappointment as each humiliating picture was erased.

"There's one more," Clay said, catching his breath. "It's in his wallet."

Diego took out Burt's wallet and removed the creased photo of the naked boy. Tears welled up in Diego's eyes at the sight. Turning his head, he looked at Burt as if he could kill him with his own bare hands.

"Please," Clay said reaching out his hand.

Diego handed the photo to Clay, who cradled it in his hand as if he had finally retrieved the last missing piece of himself.

"It's okay, Clay," Diego said. "You can go now."

Clay grabbed his duffel bag and backpack and then turned to run out the door.

"Go ahead and run," Burt said. "That's all you do! That's all you'll ever do!"

Clay stopped and looked back. "All this time you were chasing me, I may have been running from my life, but so were you, Burt. So were you."

Burt's shoulders slumped under Diego's grasp. "I'll catch up with you! The things you do, the things you've done, they don't go away. I know who you really are! I'm always going to be there to remind you. Always!!!"

As Diego held Burt off, Clay Grant ran into the night.

Ascending the mountain, Clay ran from every childhood ghost that chased him, every memory, every truth, every accusation. Burt's voice screamed in his head. If he ran any faster, his feet would take flight. Just get to the crest, over the darkened mountain, and he'll never find you! Never!

Shards of moonlight cut through the native redwoods and mighty oaks creating a path before him. Was this path from God? He didn't know, but dust and light beneath his feet led him through the maze of trees along the ridge. With each stride, it was as if the lamp's path was appearing before him and disappearing behind him.

Breathless, Clay was halfway up the blackened mountain when the forest closed in on him. Determined to make it over the crest, he pressed forward, following that light at his feet.

The moon's path verged beyond the thick brush, the familiar sound within earshot; the thunderous crash calming his panicked heart before the reality set in.

He wasn't at the crest. He was at the falls.

Surging and plunging, the rushing falls were illuminated by the moon's uninhibited light. Threads of azure blue, crystal and clear, coming to life before disappearing into the mist and darkness below. His eyes were full of desperation. The falls were all that existed in that moment. Three separate falls, brilliant and gushing, emanating from one majestic source. Echoing off the rocks, the falls were drawing him near. They were calling out his name.

*"You are my beloved son, in whom I'm well pleased."*

Was this providence or a dead end? And how could he hear the name beloved now? Gripping his duffel bag, Clay held the tattered photograph up to the night sky; the missing piece of himself, bruised and injured once more. Staring into his own eyes, he recognized the familiar terror hidden within. After all these years had nothing changed?

Clay felt a gentle mist against his face, the mighty roar of the falls, like a lion, growing fiercer. The roar calling out his name.

*"You are my beloved son, in whom I'm well pleased."*

Only now did Clay understand what the boy in that photo, his younger self, was trying to tell him. There was no other choice. Tears streaming down his face, Clay knew what he must do.

Leaving his bags on the bank, Clay climbed onto the rock formation that jetted out over the falls, the gushing current beating against his feet. Making his way across the narrow ridge, Clay slipped but recovered his balance. Kneeling on the ledge, Clay said a prayer over the photograph, an apology to the boy he could never protect; the one he neglected and refused to listen to. The one he, himself, never called beloved.

Entrusting that boy to God, Clay gently laid the photograph on the current, and let go. Making his peace, he watched the tattered photograph float away.

Clay felt a chill throughout his body. He wasn't alone.

Eyes full of rage, Burt emerged from the forest, blood on

his shirt, and his camera at his side.

Clay's first instinct was to run, but there was nowhere for him to go. Caught between Burt and the falls, he just knelt on the ridge, clinging to the rock as the rushing current crashed below.

Flashes of light enveloped him, igniting the forest.

"I can't wait for the world to see these. This is how I remember you!"

Burt climbed onto the rocks and crossed the ridge, bursts of light from his camera blinding Clay.

"Stupid boy," Burt yelled. "You are still the same!"

But Clay had made peace with the boy within. Rising to his feet, Clay faced the man who caused him so much harm. For the first time, Clay stood before him not as a boy, but as a man, absorbing the weight of his hate and resentment, doing his best to hold on to what he knew was true. Doing his best to hold onto his true name. Listening to the roar of the falls, Clay surrendered to what he could not control.

Burt moved closer. "I wonder what the world would think if they saw those photos we took?"

Aiming his camera, Burt was only a few feet from Clay when the roaring current swept against him, knocking him off balance. Hugging his camera, Burt slid down the soaked ledge, bracing himself with his foot as the falls rushed below.

"Hold on!" Clay yelled. He extended his hand but Burt wouldn't let go of the camera.

"Let go!" Clay yelled again. "Grab my hand!"

The next wave swept over the rock, enveloping Burt.

Clay's eyes widened.

Clinging to the camera, Burt separated from the ledge,

his screams echoing off the rocks and throughout the mountainside.

Arms outstretched, Burt fell backwards, disappearing into the raging falls below, the darkness consuming him.

Clay froze in disbelief. Like the fire, had he caused this?

"He slipped. I saw it myself." Diego emerged from the darkness. He had a gash on his face from where Burt hit him with his camera before getting away.

Sirens rang out. Clay panicked.

"Ted called the cops before I could stop him. He thought he was helping."

"The cops?"

Diego helped Clay jump off the rock formation and back onto the bank. Clay knew he didn't have much time. "Which way to the crest?"

"You don't have to run. I saw him fall. This wasn't your fault."

"It's all my fault!" Clay said catching his breath.

Tears in his eyes, Diego grabbed him by the shirt. "I saw that photo. Believe me, none of this is your fault. You didn't cause that. And you didn't cause this."

Sirens grew louder. Clay spotted a helicopter in the sky.

"Please, I don't have much time. I have to go!"

Against his best judgment, Diego conceded. "You're only a quarter mile from the crest. Follow that path," Diego said pointing up the hill. "I'll take care of this."

"How can I ever repay you?"

"Just stop blaming yourself."

Gathering his bags, Clay turned his attention up the hill, knowing he had to reach the other side of the mountain before morning. Clay wiped the tears from his face.

"Goodbye, my friend," Clay said.

Eyes rising to the star-filled sky, Clay ascended the mountain, determined never to return.

As Diego searched for Burt's body, Clay blended into the darkened forest.

A few moments later, two figures appeared from the brush: Reagan and Ted. Flashlights in hand, they spotted Diego along the bank of the falls, but Clay was nowhere to be found.

"It's too late," Diego said.

Reagan turned to his son. "What have I done?"

## Chapter Thirty

The High Hope sanctuary basked in the brilliant morning sun. Bells rang out as the people entered the church.

Word had gotten out about an accident up at the falls, but no one from the church knew the person's identity or connection to High Hope.

Diego had spoken to the authorities and his account was enough to rule Burt's demise an accident. Burt wasn't the first tragedy at the falls, and the town knew he wouldn't be the last.

Burt's camera was recovered five miles downstream, the lens shattered and the memory card destroyed. By daybreak, Burt's body was still not found, but that was just a matter of time. After an elder prayed for the soul of the unknown victim, Ted stepped into the pulpit.

Nervous, Ted waited as the camera readied into position. Reagan had scheduled the dedication of the memorial garden the same day, so even though they had announced that Ted was preaching in advance, the sanctuary was packed. Looking out into the crowd, Ted searched for his father.

Reagan settled into a seat in the empty balcony. He didn't want to make Ted self-conscious or take attention away from him. He thought he had slipped in unnoticed, but then he heard the familiar voice behind him.

"Can I sit with you?" The boy stood a few feet away tugging on his tie.

Normally, Reagan would insist that Tyler sit up front, but given the circumstances, he made an exception.

The staff sat together in the first few rows sharing doubtful glances as Ted's face filled the Jumbotron.

Thomas discreetly turned to the group. "Can you believe someone went over the falls last night?"

Monica replied in a whisper, "Maybe he heard Ted's sermon in advance and decided to jump?"

As the staff tried to contain their laughter, Monica made eye contact with Ted and gave him thumbs-up!

Ted scanned the crowd. Clay was nowhere to be found. He clutched the crumpled paper, filled with Clay's thoughts. Am I really going to do this? Looking up from the paper, Ted shared Clay's words.

*"It's one thing to believe in something when you don't need it to be true. It's another when everything is riding on it."*

Ted took a deep breath.

*"I've never had an accurate perception of God."*

Ted finally spotted his father in the balcony beside Tyler. He kept his eyes locked on Reagan for a moment.

*"When I was a boy, God was like a kind, yet distant grandfather. Loving, but disengaged."*

Reagan reached over and patted Tyler on the shoulder.

*"When I got older, I perceived God as an unsympathetic IRS agent fixated on my flaws and always hot on my trail."*

The congregation shared knowing smiles. Ted had made a connection.

"Apparently, I am not alone in that perception." Ted continued, a bit more confident in Clay's words,

*"How we perceive God has everything to do with how we perceive ourselves.*

*"A distant God has left me lonely and insecure. A critical and angry God has left me fearful of living. I can never please either one."*

Ted stopped and glanced at the page, realizing he wasn't the only one who felt this way.

Reagan stared at his son.

*"I've spent years numbing or outrunning those voices of condemnation that I can't get out of my head.*

All this striving and I still end up here. Lost. Alone. Drowning in expectations I can never live up to. And those voices say the same thing, 'You're not enough.'"

Clay's words caught in Ted's throat,

"If only I tried harder, they'd be happy, and she would have stayed.

"And so you put on the mask, trying to be everything to everyone. That's the trick, right? Reject yourself before you can be rejected.

"But who does God say that I am? He calls me His beloved son."

Ted continued to share Clay's words, and to his surprise, the congregation was actively engaged. The words he spoke resonated, the feelings and thoughts he always felt inside seemed to lift the words off the paper.

The staff listened intently, surprised by Ted's candor. Ted had humanity in his eyes and a passion that had been missing. The light within him shined. And besides, these words were ministering to them.

Taking a long stare at the crumpled paper, Ted delivered the final thought.

"In wearing our mask we reject our true self and betray the humanity entrusted to us."

The image of Clay's mask flashed in his mind, but instead of Clay's face, he saw his own. Ted paused and then repeated his last line, saying it for himself this time.

*"In wearing our mask we reject our true self and betray the humanity entrusted to us."*

Clay's words penetrated Ted's own heart. He stood there for a reflective moment as they sunk in.

Pushing Clay's message aside, he stepped away from the pulpit. In the stillness of the sanctuary Ted could hear his own breath.

He stood there vulnerable and transparent before the congregation. Then it happened. Ted Mitchell found his own words.

"Is it possible to be standing still and discover that you've been running all your life?

"That you're surrounded by people, but are in hiding nonetheless; unwilling to share that piece of yourself because it's just not safe.

"And how do you stop running when you're not even moving?"

Looking at the faces across the pews, he asked the question, "What do I want to hear from the pulpit? I want to hear that I am welcome. Not the person you want me to be or the person I often pretend to be but the person that I am. Is that person welcome, here at this table?"

Ted moved to the rustic communion table. It was bare, aside from the basket and ceramic cup upon the folded cloth. The carved inscription read, "Do this in remembrance of me".

He stared up into the balcony at his father and son and the jagged crack that skirted the central beam. It was what he always saw when he was in the pulpit, but somehow it meant something different to him now—as if the flaw, the imperfection were there to remind us of something.

"See, He knew we'd forget. So at this table He says, 'My children, my beloved children, remember, I was human. I was human.'"

Slowly, the congregation began to applaud. Rising to their feet, they affirmed both Ted and the message he had shared.

Tyler looked to his grandfather, surprised. "Was that my dad?"

"Yep, that's my son."

"I wish my mom could have seen this."

Reagan patted Tyler on the shoulder. "We'll send her the DVD."

✳

Immediately following the service, Ted received a crowd that waited in line to congratulate him, but was unaffected by the praise. For the first time it just felt good to be comfortable in his skin. It wasn't that he was ungrateful. He just realized that this wasn't about him or, at least, not him alone. With each handshake and hug, he felt a connection with the people that he had never experienced before. It was an acknowledgement of each other's humanity and a quiet promise to never forget again. Or at least to try not to.

Tyler cut through the line and stood proudly by his father's side.

Ted put his arm around his son's shoulders. He knew what Tyler would be thinking: that somehow because he'd done well that his mother would come back. Ted knew he would have to talk to him sooner than later.

Reagan remained in the empty balcony. The dedication would begin soon, but he wanted to wait as long as he could to give his son his moment in the spotlight. Pulling back the tattered curtain over the stained glass window in the back of the balcony, he squinted as the sun poured in. He was missing Rose but as he stared at his son below, it was like a piece of her was there.

The staff looked on in amazement.

"That wasn't the Ted I know," Max said discreetly to the other staff members.

"I didn't know he had it in him," Alexis replied.

"I didn't know he had anything in him," Monica said giving thumbs-up to Ted in the distance.

"Are you still leaving?" Thomas asked Monica.

"Hell, yes," Monica said. "This week the crowd is waving palm branches, next week they could just as easily crucify him. Honestly, what are the odds that he can keep this up?"

"You're probably right," Max conceded, but couldn't help admitting to himself that he was inspired by what he had witnessed.

Harper, an elder and organizer of the church's annual golf tournament, approached Max. He was carrying a clipboard. "We still don't have a Chairman for the High Hope Golf Classic. I was hoping we could count on you." Harper held out the clipboard to Max.

"That's not until spring, right?" Alexis asked, knowing of

Max's plan to leave.

Tyler was milling the crowd looking for Clay.

"Hey, Tyler," Max called out. "I need a caddie. Are you interested?"

"Can I drive the cart?"

"We'll talk." Max signed his name as Alexis and the rest of staff looked on in amazement.

Ted was distracted as he continued to receive people. He was looking expectantly into the crowd as his dad approached.

Reagan smiled with pride at Ted's success, trying not to gloat about being right about Clay and Ted.

Ted smirked, realizing that his father was either brilliant or incredibly lucky, probably a combination of both. He discreetly whispered to his father, "Did you find him?"

Reagan looked to Diego who was standing several feet away.

Diego shook his head no.

"Do you think he's gone for good?" Ted asked his father.

"I don't know. I don't know."

&#42;

The dedication of the memorial garden had come to an end. It was late afternoon and everyone had cleared out.

The High Hope truck rumbled as Diego pulled into the upper church parking lot. As he rounded the bend, he spotted Ted and Tyler having a conversation in the distance.

As Diego hopped out of the truck, the boy walked toward him gripping a wrinkled tie in his hand. All the joy at seeing his father succeed had evaporated. Diego crouched down beside him.

"What's wrong, Tyler?"

"My mom's not coming back. My dad just told me."

"Did you think she might?"

"I just thought if my dad did a really good job...." The boy caught himself. "Clay was right; it doesn't work that way. I know it's not my fault, but I wish I could fix it."

"What I like about you, Tyler, is that you just keep going."

"Clay didn't even say goodbye."

"He was your friend, wasn't he?"

"Yeah," Tyler sighed. "Why does everybody leave, Diego?"

"Just know that no matter whoever comes and whoever goes, you're never going to be alone. Why don't you help me unload the truck, and then we can go to the Acorn and get some dessert."

Tyler tossed his tie in the back of the truck and hoisted himself up. Looking in the bed of the truck, he discovered a duffel bag. The boy's mouth fell open in amazement.

"Have you ever had Tiramisu?" Diego grinned.

＊

Sunday nights were quiet at the Acorn. The breakfast crowd was long gone and those who stopped by after the dedication had returned to their homes and families.

The counter was empty. The rustic faces of city workers and ranch hands depicted in the art-deco mural were like guardians keeping watch over the town; the bold colors and idealistic message of brotherhood were more apparent in the stillness.

Becky was putting out the set-ups for the next day. She stared at the spoon, watching the colorful light from the cellophane toothpicks overhead dancing in the reflection.

"The owner just called. There is a private party here tonight," the waitress said to Becky. "Would you work it?"

Becky glanced at the clock. Her shift was ending soon, but it wasn't like she had any real plans. "Sure."

She had a standing invitation for dinner at her brother's but that was his family time. Besides she didn't want to hear about whatever plans they had for moving to Chicago.

Tossing the rag on the counter, Becky stepped into the kitchen and was surprised by what she discovered.

Clay stood in the doorway holding two grocery bags and a bouquet of sunflowers.

Becky didn't know if she could trust what she was looking at. "What are you doing here?"

"I got as far as North Beach. And then I realized you've never had Tiramisu. It just didn't seem right."

Clay managed to hand Becky the sunflowers. "These are for you. They're a pitiful bunch, really."

Becky looked them over.

"I just had a feeling that in the right hands they might have a shot." Clay set the bags on the counter. "I got everything we need." Reaching into the bag, he removed each item he had purchased at the Italian store in the city. "Flour, the good kind, coffee beans for the espresso, cocoa powder and brandy. The right ingredients matter if you're going to make the real thing."

"And you plan on making all this here?"

"I have permission." He grinned.

Looking over her shoulder, Becky saw the waitresses gathered about, smiling.

"And most importantly, we have the right recipe." Clay tore a piece of the brown paper bag with the recipe scribbled in pencil. "I called a special friend and she convinced her dad to give it to me."

"A special friend?" Becky squinted, looking suspect.

"Don't worry, Bella's only ten. By the way, she says hello."

"You told her about me?"

"Yeah, and she gave me some good advice. Actually, something I had told her. I'd repeat it but it really doesn't make any sense unless you're hanging from a rope."

Becky rolled her eyes. "Just because we have the right recipe and the right ingredients, it still doesn't mean it's going to turn out all right."

"There is so much about me that I'm afraid that once you find out you're not going to like. But this time I'm here to stay."

"You're not going to disappear on me?"

"I have some unfinished business in Kansas, only a couple of days, but then I'll be back. It's time to make peace with my mom. Someone told me, 'It's important to find the words while they can still do some good.'"

"What are you going to tell her?"

"All is forgiven. Forgive me. Forgive yourself."

Becky's eyes welled up with tears. "Don't tell me how, but I knew you'd come back."

"How could you know? You don't really know me," Clay said, puzzled.

"Maybe I know you better than you think."

"I'm sorry I didn't tell you—"

"I'm only interested in the real Clay," Becky said. "I want you to stay, but will you be safe if the paparazzi comes back?"

"It doesn't matter. It finally occurred to me, they're not looking for me. They're looking for 'Little Guy Mike,' or who they need me to be, and that's not me.

"I don't know what is going to happen, but sometimes that's all you get in life. Like you said, those little glimpses of Heaven. I've missed too many of those."

He held up the wooden spoon. "Bake with me?"

The "Closed" sign sat in the window at the Acorn. Whatever threat was out there, Clay was no longer going to waste his life running.

Clay and Becky were covered in cocoa powder, laughing as they stood before the stainless steel bowl. As she held the wooden spoon, he reached around and placed his hand over hers, and then guided her as she folded the egg whites into the mascarpone mixture.

Glancing at the rustic faces in the mural and the promise hidden in their eyes, he was still unable to reconcile the idealistic message of brotherhood with the truth about the paintings in the barn.

"What is it?" Becky said, noticing the curious expression on his face.

"I wish I could sit down with the artist who painted that mural. I think I could learn a lot from him."

"But you know the artist."

Looking more closely this time, he spotted something he had missed before. The artist's mark was in the lower right hand corner: "DXM."

He had seen those initials before. "Of course, Diego..."

In that moment Clay knew he was exactly where he was supposed to be. Despite everything that had or would happen, he was staying put. That much he knew.

He glanced at the cellophane toothpicks overhead. It was a glimpse of Heaven.

✳

# *Epilogue*

Sunflowers sat in a vase on the counter and draped over the fresh tray of Tiramisu, which was absorbing the brandy.

Clay took Becky's hand and spun her around before embracing her and settling into a slow dance as Patsy Cline played on the radio.

Peering through the window, a woman watched from outside the diner. The mystery was solved. The address in her hand was right. Although she hadn't seen her son since he was a teenager, she couldn't mistake him. Or those eyes. He was beautiful. Catching her breath, she watched as Clay embraced the girl he was with, smiling in a way she had forgotten he could. Tears streaming down Patty's face, she knew that this was enough. It was enough to know he was safe. That he was happy. More than enough and more than she could ever expect. She didn't have the right to disrupt his life now. Not after what she had done. And what would she say? Maybe one day she would find the words but for now this was enough.

Turning to leave, Patty let out a deep breath, a cloud of

darkness lifting from her shoulders. At least she would always be able to remember him smiling. Praying that she would see her son again, she stepped off the curb and into the waiting taxi.

As the taxi drove away, the cabbie asked, "Back to the airport already? Most people stay long enough to see the falls."

"Are there *really* falls in Cliff Falls?"

"Absolutely. They're beautiful but also dangerous. Some photographer fell to his death last night."

"A photographer?"

"People are always having accidents up there or getting lost searching for the falls. Me? I'd rather spend my time in the green valley, in an open space along one of the healthy streams or gentle brooks. If you think about it, that water has gone through a lot of trouble to forge a path down the mountain. The mighty falls have emptied themselves, humbled themselves to come to you." He glanced into the rearview mirror, "That's the great thing about the falls. Sooner or later, they come to you."

Looking out the window, Patty thought of her son. *Sooner or later, they come to you.* She fought back tears. "God, I hope so."

As the taxi made its way down the mountain, Cliff Falls faded in the distance. Patty Grant gazed at the star-filled sky believing that she would see her boy again.

It was hope's first breath.

*Beyond the Falls*

# Acknowledgments

This is a book about belief, so it is only fitting that I thank all of those who were not only a part of this project, but who believed in this story–and in me. Talented people with generous hearts, they are but a few of the faces that I see in the mural above the counter at the Acorn. I am proud to walk among them.

At age 26, I went over the falls in my own life when a health challenge landed me in bed with little more to do than write. Cliff Falls was part of my restoration and was years in the making.

This novel would not exist without my mom, Marie Anne Shiepe. From day one, she believed that I could do it, and that it would be healing for others who read it. Her gift of belief is unending and allows all those around her to believe in a loving God. I am grateful for her support, and for the continued support of my father, Clifford Shiepe, my sister, Bayne, and brother-in-law, Jose Meza.

Nancy Ellen Dodd has been my trusted editor for every phase of this project. A talented writer herself, she has an amazing ability to take my words and arrange them in an unexpected ways. I am grateful for her friendship.

Jeremy Rivera is a brother and a best friend. A gifted speaker, he paints with words and calls people to a more sincere walk with God. He pours his heart into everything he does and has been a sounding board for the book and my life. One real friend is worth a thousand imitations.

Maureen Saliba has a gift for logic and believability that I relied on throughout this project–often that included endlessly reading passages over the phone until we were both confused. Whatever challenge was before me, she never hesitated to jump in and to see if she could help. That's the kind of person she is.

Jo Lynn Bolton's respect for the creative process is inspiring. We spent countless hours reviewing chapters, and she listened patiently as I explored every imaginable option. She always treated my ideas and manuscript with reverence, which is how she treats everyone in her life.

Paul Petersen shared insight that could only have come from a former child star, bringing new life to my manuscript. Chip Flaherty saw this as a movie from the start. The late Ron Glosser, my mentor and friend, with his wife, Lily, always did everything they could to encourage me. Thanks to Auntie Sandie, for her never-ending belief. Brian Hill, for Sunday dinner on the farm. And to Evelyn Freed who believes in the power of the Arts to heal.

I want to acknowledge my team of first readers: My friend and childhood priest, the Most Rev. Nicholas Samra, Devon Parisi, Tima Parvaresh, Joe Thackwell, Lannette Turicchi, Adetayo West and Jen Yuan.

Mark Yameen, for his Boston Strong support; Michael Marchand, who always told me to keep writing; Action Hero Jorgen De Mey, who was part of my physical restoration that shadowed the writing process; Kevin Collins, who was there at the start; Louis and Natalia Pastis, for their encouragement; Greg Parker, who was always invested in the process; and Linda Summers, who reminded me that God wasn't done with Cliff Falls.

Thank you to the good people at The Dutch Goose, the Fisherman's Feast and Mike's Pastry who gave me permission to use them in the novel, to Michelle Katz from Art Center College of Design, and to Jane Strauss, my high school English teacher, for inspiring her students to write.

A special thank you to Amy Grant, whose voice and lyrics have ministered to me, reminding me what is real, and to the late Brennan Manning for daring us to trust that God loves us as we are and not as we should be. To the remarkable Leslie Fram for simply being remarkable. Thank you for shining your spotlight on Cliff Falls. And to Allison Hill, an independent author's best friend.

Thanks to my creative team: Sean Teegarden and Jane Moon for the inspired cover design; Soo Kim for her thoughtful interior layout; and Pam McComb for my cover photo. I appreciate all of their time and dedication.

Above all, I want to thank the One who has seen me through. "After you have suffered a little while, He Himself will restore you and make you strong, firm and steadfast." – 1 Peter 5:10. Whatever that looks like, I'm game.

## *Continue the Journey*
at CLIFFFALLS.COM

**Discover** more about *Cliff Falls*
and find out what others are saying.

Find out the **latest news** about *Cliff Falls*,
including author events and appearances.

**Download** Reader Group Discussion
Questions and Clay's Journal.

Purchase additional copies of *Cliff Falls*.
**Exclusive** discounts on orders of six or more.

*Cliff Falls* IS **NOW AVAILABLE** ON AUDIBLE!

---

## *Share the Experience*

The touchstone of the *Cliff Falls* **experience**
comes full circle when you invite others into it.

**Review** *Cliff Falls* on:
Amazon and Goodreads

**Follow** us on:

ⓕ CLIFFFALLS    ⓨ CLIFFFALLSBOOK
ⓘ CLIFFFALLS    ▶ CLIFFFALLSMEDIA

For information about having the author speak
to your group or organization, please contact:

OFFICE@CLIFFFALLS.COM

# Clay's Journal

**GOING DEEPER**: A PERSONAL JOURNALING EXERCISE

---

Often, God speaks in a "still small voice." That's when Clay would hear from Him. And journaling was how he was able to make and keep that connection. Below is a list of quotes. Don't worry about punctuation or sounding eloquent. Just meditate on the quote and prompt, and then write the first thing that comes to mind. Like the road to the falls, you may be surprised to find where it leads.

**DAY 1 (COURAGE):**

> *"Scared children—all of us—dealing with adult things—wondering if we are that strong. And everyone wants us to be someone or something else."*

**Everyone struggles with fear. What specific fears are holding you back, and how can you walk through them?**

**DAY 2 (BROKENNESS):**

> *"What is needed is the humanity of someone who has been broken, someone like you."*

**The world values strength, but what are some ways God can use your specific brokenness (hurts, pain, mistakes)?**

**DAY 3 (TRUE SELF):**

> *"In wearing our mask we reject our true self and betray the humanity entrusted to us."*

**In what ways do you reject your true self? How does this affect your relationships with yourself, others, and God?**

## DAY 4 (ACCEPTANCE):

*"Until you showed up, I never knew I was waiting to be found. And you didn't come after 'Little Guy Mike.' You came after me. I guess I've been waiting my whole life for someone to come after me."*

**When have you felt loved and accepted for being the real you? How did it affect you? What does that show you about God's love?**

## DAY 5 (MEMORIES):

*"Memories could be as powerful as the words that accompanied them, both capable of erasing the distance time had put in place."*

**How is "remembering" both a blessing and a curse? What is the difference between facing the past and dwelling in the past?**

## DAY 6 (GIFTS AND TALENTS):

*"God has given you a gift with words. I'd rather you try and fail than sit on the sidelines. You've sat on the sidelines too long."*

**We are all given gifts and talents. What are yours? How are you using those talents? What areas in your life are you sitting on the sidelines and need to get back in the game?**

## DAY 7 (HOPE):

*"Clay stared at the gilded crucifix above the altar; it was Hope taking its last breath."*

**Describe a situation that you dreaded but turned out better than you could have thought or imagined.**

## DAY 8 (MAKING AMENDS):

*"It's important to find the words while they can still do some good."*

**How do you find the right words? To whom do you need to say them?**

**DAY 9 (FAITH):**

> *"With each step he was increasingly aware of the determined eyes as the rays continued to seep in through the splintered wood. For a moment he couldn't tell if the light was pouring in or pouring out."*

**When was the last time you felt like you were stepping on holy ground? How did it impact you? Have you ever reasoned that it might all be holy ground?**

**DAY 10 (LOVE):**

> *"I was twelve when I first realized that all the people-pleasing in the world would never make them love me or make my mom come back."*

**What are the dangers of people pleasing? Should you give of yourself without expecting anything back? And how do you get love if you don't people please?**

**DAY 11 (RECONCILIATION):**

> *"There's a difference between doing something bad and believing you are bad. God did not create you to hate yourself. It takes courage to believe that you are the beloved of God."*

**Do you know the difference between doing something bad and believing you are bad? How do you come to realize that you are truly known and loved by God?**

**DAY 12 (TRANSFORMATION):**

> *"The only words that matter are the ones that flow from the cracks in our spirit, through the breaches in our resolve."*

**How have you experienced the power of the right words being said to you? If so, what did it lead you to do? How did it change you?**

---

Visit **CLIFFFALLS.COM** for the complete journal and questions.

## Discussion Questions

1. With which character do you most identify?

2. Clay battles with trust all his life. Who are the people that Clay trusts without reservation and why? Does he trust himself?

3. Clay refuses to open his journal and yet cannot throw it away. Why?

4. Burt was Clay's "tormentor" and now relentlessly pursues him. He is the "voice of the accuser". How do bullies shape our lives? How do we begin to erase the lies they write on our hearts? What about lies that have an element of truth?

5. When Clay arrives in Cliff Falls, Reagan gives him an assignment that causes him to struggle with his authentic self and become transparent. He must enter all his pain, and his past, and risk being overwhelmed by them to find the words. Why doesn't he just run?

6. There are parallels between Clay (the child star) and Ted (the pastor's kid). How are they alike in their struggles and realizations? Were they both exploited? How are they both brave? What about Tyler?

7. What is Diego's purpose in Cliff Falls? What is the significance that the paintings were hidden within the weathered barn? How do we hide our own suffering and why?

8. *Page 201*. Clay is just looking for "the real thing," whether that is Tiramisu or a relationship. When Clay meets Becky he describes what he sees in her eyes as "...hope dwelling in a place of sadness." What is he talking about and why is Becky drawn to him?

9. The Acorn Diner is symbolically significant. It is located between the city below and the church further up the hill. To Becky the counter is holy. "People who would never interact outside of this place, taking time to come together, share a bit of their lives." What does it mean to Clay to have a seat at the counter? Where is your Acorn Diner?

10. Besides Clay, how are the following characters running? Bella, Tyler, Ted, Reagan and Burt?

11. *Page 226.* "You are my beloved son, in whom I am well pleased." When Clay hears these unexpected words, he immediately flashes back to painful childhood memories. He began to sob and his mask was stripped away. How does repeating this phrase change his view of himself and others?

12. *Page 252.* Clay's mother is still making money off her son, selling items similar to the ones Clay destroyed in the fire. Why is she selling them and what is the real reason the "Highest Bidder" is buying them?

13. *Page 266.* "In wearing our mask we reject our true self and betray the humanity entrusted to us." What truth does this hold for you?

14. *Page 231.* The falls are hard to find. The signs are hard to see. And Clay even doubted their existence. When Clay was ready to find the falls, he discovered them by wandering and listening. What did Clay discover about himself at the falls? If you've ever "gone over the falls" in your own life, what did you discover about yourself?

C.B. Shiepe's award-winning novel – *Cliff Falls* –
reaches a broad audience and resonates with readers
who have gone over the falls in their own lives. Shiepe
has garnered much media attention, appearing
on NBC, PBS, TBN, *Hour of Power*, in *Guideposts
Magazine*, at the LA Times Festival of Books, and at
speaking engagements across the country, including
the Betty Ford Center in Rancho Mirage, CA, where
actors performed scenes from his novel.

For information about having the author speak
to your group or organization, please contact:

OFFICE@CLIFFFALLS.COM